MW01232802

Totally Sarah

Totally Sarah

Extra Sensory Perception
leads a young Canadian girl
into and out of danger

Gladys Dorris

Library of Congress Control Number: 2013905844
ISBN: Hardcover   978-1-4836-1813-5
               Softcover   978-1-4836-1812-8
               Ebook   978-1-4836-1814-2

This book was printed in the United States of America.

Rev. date: 08/15/2013

To order additional copies of this book, contact:
Xlibris LLC
1-888-795-4274
www.Xlibris.com
Orders@Xlibris.com
128507

CONTENTS

Short Story

This book is dedicated in memory of Verna Linna "Jack" Dorris, who was the best mother-in-law in the world. Jack always encouraged me to write. She made me promise her that I would write after I retired from teaching. I thank her for that. Jack was an avid reader; she enjoyed reading an entire book every day the last ten to possibly fifteen years of her life when her health began to fail.

It is also dedicated to a very special woman, Silvia Striegler, my librarian and teacher friend, who has always enthusiastically encouraged me and everyone around her. I admire her quiet strength, wisdom, and determination. Silvia has influenced me in many, many ways. Thank you, Silvia.

Cover model is Sydney Frook, the author's great niece.

Since *Totally Sarah* is set in Canada, British spellings have been used throughout the novel.

Characters, addresses, and events depicted in both the novel and the short story are fictional.

CHAPTER 1

The Lady in Red

The sickening smell of vomit filled the child's bedroom as overwhelming nausea tormented her small body. Sarah Johnson's legs pulled up in the fetal position as she trembled beneath fresh linens and retched repeatedly, uncontrollably into the large yellow Tupperware bowl her mother held. She threw up continuously until there was nothing left in her to expel, and her body continued to jerk painfully for several more minutes.

"It's all right, baby. Let it all out so you can rest," Ruby assured her eight-year-old daughter and hoped that her voice concealed her trepidation. She needed to believe that Sarah would get better. This was the third day her precious little girl's fever hovered around thirty-two degrees Celsius.

Ruby's whole demeanor showed the strain of worry—creases framed her light-blue eyes, and her lips pressed together forming an almost straight line. She wore no makeup, and her long brown disheveled hair hung in matted clumps, resembling a cocker spaniel. Her shoulders drooped from sheer exhaustion, but she refused to sleep.

This was Wednesday, and yesterday, old Dr. Timmons had muttered something about an unusual strain of influenza and possible brain damage caused by the fever before he placed a bottle of pills on the kitchen table and left their house. He resented making house calls, but he told himself that the family could not afford a hospital stay where Sarah could receive the necessary intravenous body fluids she desperately needed. The truth was that he did not want to be bothered on his only day off duty. Dr. Timmons decided that Sarah was not yet dangerously dehydrated and promised himself that he would check on her progress in a couple of days. Right now, he was heading back to his recliner and afternoon glass of brandy.

Ruby sat stoically on the bed beside her little girl and noted the changes in her normally effervescent, extroverted child. *It was only four days ago that we had so much fun at the zoo,* she thought as she fluffed the pillow beneath her tiny blond head. Sarah and her younger brother, James, always enjoyed going to the local petting zoo in London. Ruby closed her eyes and prayed silently, fervently for her daughter's recovery. Despite Dr. Timmons's diagnosis, Ruby feared losing Sarah.

Sarah's frail frame revealed that she was somewhat emaciated, and her dark-ringed, sunken blue eyes suggested that she might be near death. The room swirled like a wild roller-coaster ride as she clung tightly to her pillow and mattress, fearing that she would spin off the bed into an unfamiliar white place she didn't want to go. The retching eased slowly and finally ceased as a blanket of peaceful oblivion carried her back into restful unconsciousness.

This was the closest Sarah could come to the healing sleep she so desperately needed. She had floated in and out of consciousness repeatedly since the onset of her illness. Fifteen minutes of violent nausea, followed by roughly half an hour of sleep resembling unconsciousness, then more nausea and more unconsciousness, over and over again, forming a pattern Sarah seemed destined to repeat forever. *Sarah can't take much more of this,* Ruby thought, *and neither can I.* She had gone without rest herself for over a hundred hours now, and her body ached for some deep REM sleep.

Ruby stayed in the child's room, watching Sarah's chest rise and fall in shallow breaths, holding the yellow bowl on her lap as she subconsciously rocked slowly in the antique wooden rocker by the bed. Occasionally, her head dropped briefly in fitful sleep and jerked suddenly alert with every movement in the bed. About three hours into the fourth day, Ruby's eyes flew open to find Sarah standing in front of her. Sarah's eyes were open yet unconnected to the child's brain; she was standing but still asleep. In this sleepwalking state, Sarah turned and walked slowly into the attached bathroom, lifted the drinking glass beside the sink as though she wanted a drink of water, but she didn't turn on the faucet. Instead, she lifted the glass high above her head and flung it hard across the room, smashing it on the ceramic tile floor, sending shards of glass throughout the small room. Then she simply turned and went back to bed as though nothing unusual had happened. Somehow she avoided stepping on any pieces of glass as she headed back to bed.

Sarah slept softly but fitfully the remainder of the night while her mother swept up the pieces of glass and returned to her bedside chair. Subconsciously, Ruby appreciated the respite. For just a few minutes, she had something to do other than worrying.

A beam of morning sunlight woke Sarah. She glanced at her sleeping mother. Sheer exhaustion and early morning quiet had dragged Ruby unwillingly into slumber; she slept sitting straight up in the rocking chair, still holding the yellow bowl on her lap. Since Sarah did not feel the immediate urge to throw up, she decided to let her mother rest a little longer.

The child intuitively sensed that someone else was in the room, watching, studying her. She directed her attention toward the foot of the bed and wondered who the very pretty, dark-haired young lady dressed all in red and seated on the foot of her bed was. She didn't remember ever meeting the woman before. Sarah noted her thick, long dark wavy hair, piercing brown eyes, long dark eyelashes, and vivid red lipstick. The woman smiled quietly, revealing an even row of pearlescent white teeth, but she didn't speak for several minutes. Sarah was not frightened, but instead, she felt strangely comforted.

"Do not be afraid, Sarah. You are going to be okay." The lady's soft soothing voice sounded oddly familiar to Sarah. She closed her eyes as a sudden wave of nausea engulfed her, and Ruby sprang into action with the bowl. The vomiting seemed to take several minutes but in reality lasted only two. When the retching stopped, Sarah looked again toward the foot of her bed, but there was no one there.

"Where did the woman go, Mom? Who is she?" Sarah asked.

"What woman, honey? I am the only one here." Sarah told her mother all about the lady in red, and Ruby listened but didn't believe. *She must be hallucinating because of the fever,* Ruby thought but didn't say. Ruby didn't notice the slight indentation in the crumpled bedding at the foot of her child's bed, but Sarah did. Unaware that her mother didn't believe the visitor was real, Sarah didn't see any need to call her mother's attention to the smooth indentation on her chenille bedspread.

Her eyes felt heavy, and she drifted back to sleep. While she slept, her fever broke and nausea lifted; Sarah did not vomit again. Later that day, she woke up hungry. The sickness was gone, and no one mentioned the lady in red again.

CHAPTER 2

The Voice

James and Sarah loved playing in the piles of brightly coloured maple leaves their father, Ken, raked and piled for them. Sometimes they used the leaves to form walls creating a pretend house, Sarah's favourite activity. James especially loved to use the pile as a makeshift cushion to soften his landing when he jumped out of the tree, yelling, "Banzai!"

One afternoon while James was banzai leaping, Sarah busied herself with building a minicastle in the sandbox. Suddenly, Sarah dropped the small blue plastic shovel when her attention was drawn toward the neighbour's ground-floor bedroom window about twenty yards east of James' leaf pile. She sensed that something serious was happening behind the closed curtain.

As if in a trance, the child sat perfectly still for nearly ten minutes, eyes transfixed on the window, her delicate right hand cupping her chin like a small *Thinker* statue. Sarah waited.

James didn't notice. He was engulfed in his own imagination.

"What are you doing, sis?" In his estimation, he had just performed the perfect skydive and landing and wanted her to tell him so. "You didn't even watch! What's going on?"

"Mr. Nolan just died," she announced in a monotone matter-of-fact tone. "I watched him go to heaven." She lifted her shovel and quietly resumed castle building.

*   *   *

One month later, Sarah knew when the mother of her school playmate and best friend Shirley died. Sarah quietly abandoned her leaf house and announced to her mother that Mrs. Monroe, who lived five blocks away, had gone to heaven. Ruby had been busy baking a date-custard pie, Sarah's favourite, and slowly wiped the flour from her hands. "What are you talking about, Sarah? I talked to Mary this morning. She was fine." Ruby's best friend,

Mary Monroe, had been battling pancreatic cancer for several months, but she seemed to be on the road to recovery. Ruby didn't believe her daughter until the phone rang and confirmed that, indeed, Mrs. Monroe had died a few minutes earlier.

Ruby stared disbelieving at her little girl. *How did she know?* she thought. *Somebody must have told her.*

"It's okay, Mommy. She's gone to heaven. I saw her go with the angels." Sarah assumed that everybody saw the angels. For her, it was just another ordinary day.

Ruby could not accept what her child was saying, so she chose to deliberately ignore it and attributed it to childhood imagination. She also ignored the haunting suspicion that Dr. Timmons's brain-damage comment might be a reality.

*   *   *

Several months passed without any more unsettling pronouncements from Sarah. The family was going Christmas shopping in London, and Sarah could not contain her excitement. She had saved her allowance for two months and wanted to get something special for Mommy, Daddy, and James. Her excitement grew as they neared downtown. Glistening clean snow blanketed the fields, houses, and stores while darker dirty snowbanks lined the plowed roads, curbs, and shoveled sidewalks. Christmas decorations flickered and danced in the chilly Canadian wind, but it was not snowing. Sarah preferred to not be riding in the car when it was snowing.

As Ruby stopped at one of the many downtown red lights, Sarah suddenly said, "Be careful, Mommy. The man in that red car is going to die," and she pointed a tiny index finger in front of her. Before Ruby could respond, a small red oncoming car ran the light and was T-boned by a delivery truck coming from Ruby's left. The red car stopped rolling inches from Ruby's front bumper, and she found herself face-to-face with the twisted, bloodied, obviously dead man. Ruby didn't notice as Sarah's eyes traced the path of something invisible rising up from the wrecked vehicle toward the clouds.

Ruby wasn't sure which frightened her more, staring into the cold eyes of the newly deceased or the realization that her little girl knew what was going to happen before it actually happened. Just like she knew when her friend Mary died, this was unbelievable. Ruby couldn't ignore it anymore. "Sarah, how did you know?" her voice betrayed her fear.

"A voice in my head told me, Mommy. I think she's my angel. Don't you have an angel too?" Ruby didn't know what to say, so again, she fell silent.

*   *   *

That evening, as Ruby tucked Sarah into bed, she decided to question her a little further. "Honey, how long have you heard the woman's voice in your head?"

"Ever since I was really sick, Mommy. You remember the lady in red I told you about? I think it's her voice that I hear." Sarah didn't mean to upset her mother. She was simply answering the question.

"Honey, I don't want you to listen to the voice anymore. I want you to tell it to stop talking to you. Okay?" Ruby recalled the doctor's words, and it scared her even more.

What if my baby is mentally disturbed now? she silently worried.

"Okay, Mommy. I'll tell her to stop." Ruby hoped that was all it would take. She had no idea that it was just the beginning.

CHAPTER 3

Great-Aunt Melissa

Lake Ontario called to Sarah and James; winds whispered the call, and seagulls cried for them to come out and play. The lake's choppy waters sang to the children, "Come out, come out, come out!" Summer vacation was nearly over and, already, the lake's cool, almost cold, spray suggested that winter would soon arrive, but the children didn't seem to notice. They enjoyed every minute spent splashing barefoot in the shallow rocky water behind Great-Aunt Melissa's house.

The family had been at Melissa's lakeside house just outside Wellington, Ontario, for two weeks. In Sarah's estimation, Great-Aunt Melissa was really old and really wrinkled; she had long, thin grey hair that touched the floor whenever she took it out of the bun at the back of her neck. She never smiled and sometimes smelled bad. She was definitely not one of Sarah's favourite relatives, but Sarah did love her grandmother, and Granny now lived with her sister, Great-Aunt Melissa.

Melissa never spoke to the children because she didn't like children. She especially didn't like children in her home. If the children were sleeping, she tolerated their presence. Otherwise, she wanted them outdoors. Melissa never even wanted them eating at her table and often exiled them, hotdog in hand, to the backyard. With the lake only twenty yards from her back door, she usually got what she wanted.

Sarah and James loved the lake and welcomed every opportunity to get clear of Great-Aunt Melissa's cold, hard stares. The backyard was lined with rosebushes on both sides with only green grass in between, literally providing a green-carpeted inviting path to the shoreline where the carpet dropped sharply to the water's edge about four feet below. To three-feet-tall children, the drop represented a virtual cliff. They both loved the gravel-covered cliff and the cool shallow water.

Since Sarah was now nine years old, she usually took the lead as director of play. She decided when and for how long they would skip rocks on the lake's surface, collect unusual-coloured rocks, hand-fish, create pretend boats with driftwood, send bottle messages to faraway places, play mermaid and sailor, or just sit quietly listening to the seagulls.

Since both children knew how to swim and always kept their bright-orange lightweight lifesaver vests on at all times, Ruby wasn't overly worried about them. She did, however, keep the door and double windows at the back of the house open whenever the children went out to play. She could clearly hear them laughing and enjoying themselves, literally, from sunup to sundown. Her biggest concerns were sunburn and rock blisters. By the end of two weeks, Sarah and James were pink tanned, freckled, and peeling, and their hair was sun bleached two shades lighter.

When Ruby tucked them into the bunk beds at night, the children were often asleep even before she kissed their rosy, sun-warmed foreheads. Sarah slept in the upper bunk, and James preferred the bottom one. The children slept in the only upstairs room at the top of the long, narrow thirteen-step stairwell. Something about the stairs made Sarah uncomfortable. She usually wasted no time getting to the top or the bottom as quickly as possible; her feet rarely touched the steps more than four times per flight.

Granny kissed and tucked them in at bedtime, their thirteenth evening at Great-Aunt Melissa's. "Good night, children. I love you both very much. Sleep tight," Granny whispered. "And don't let the bedbugs bite," she teased and left the bedroom door open as she left. As usual, the children fell immediately into deep, fun-fueled, exhausted sleep. Ruby didn't come up that night but stayed downstairs with Melissa who hadn't been feeling well since supper.

*   *   *

The room was bathed in velvet blackness when Sarah opened her eyes even though the full moon seemed close enough to be touched just outside the bedroom window. Sarah lay still and strained her eyes to make out the objects in the room—the four-drawer oak dresser with the antique bull's-eye coal-oil lamp on top, the cherrywood rocking chair at the foot of the bunk beds, the small multicoloured braided rug beside the bed, the suitcase on the floor behind the half-opened door, and two extra blankets folded on the nightstand in case the children got too cool.

Sarah bolted up, suddenly alert, and, in one smooth movement, swung her small feet dangling over the edge, sitting, waiting for something to happen. Just as suddenly, all the objects in the room disappeared into the scariest, deepest blackness Sarah had ever experienced in her short life, even blacker than when she was blindfolded during her birthday party's pin-the-tail-on-the-donkey game. The room felt as cold as the day she went with her mom to the local butcher's walk-in freezer.

"James," her voice quivered when she whispered his name. "James," she called his name again, this time a little louder. "Wake up! Something is really wrong!" By this time she was yelling, but James did not respond. She could hear him snoring softly below her.

Then the bed began to shake, slowly, almost imperceptibly at first. Sarah wondered if it was her imagination. She sat perfectly still, trying to make the bed stop moving. Suddenly, it began shaking so hard that Sarah feared she would fall off the bed. The wooden headboard beat against the wall, and Sarah wondered how James could still be sleeping.

Sarah knew something really bad was in the room with her even though she was too young to comprehend evil. She knew she had to get out and get out fast. On all fours, she quickly scampered to the headboard, reached out, grabbed the door, flung it all the way open, yelled "James" one last time, and jumped as far as she could from the still-shaking bed, landing at the top of the stairwell. Without looking back, she topped three steps, landed hard at the bottom, and kept running.

"Mom! Mom!" she ran screaming to her parents' room. "Wake up, Mom! Wake up! Something really bad is in our room, and James is still up there! Please help him! He won't wake up!" Ruby knew something was terribly wrong. She had never seen her little girl so terrified.

"Run in and stay with Granny, honey. I'll go up and get your brother." Sarah dashed across the hall to Granny's room, jumped into her bed, and pulled the covers over her head like a frightened turtle retreats into its shell. Ruby turned on the stairwell light and hurried upstairs. She found James sleeping, snoring softly in his lower bunk. Soft moonlight filled the room, and nothing appeared to be out of place. "What on earth scared Sarah so much?" she wondered. "Whatever it was, James didn't see or hear it." Puzzled, Ruby stayed in the room for several minutes.

When Ruby came back downstairs, she looked in on Sarah and found her sleeping peacefully next to Granny. Ruby decided to leave Sarah in Granny's bed for the rest of the night. She noticed the time on Granny's bedside clock; it was 3:30 a.m. She hurried back to bed for four more hours of sleep.

*   *   *

When Granny's alarm rang at seven thirty, she was surprised to find her granddaughter snuggling next to her. "Morning glory," she whispered and kissed the child gently on her forehead. Sarah looked so beautiful and innocent as she slept, Granny could not keep from smiling; she did not want to wake her sleeping beauty. Quietly, she slipped out of bed and into her robe and slippers. As usual, Granny's first official act of the day was to wake her sister, Melissa. "Rise and shine, Melissa." Her lilting voice sounded more like singing than talking. "Melissa, wake up. It's time to start our day. What would you like for breakfast?"

Melissa did not respond. When Granny pulled back the sheet, Melissa's opened eyes stared without sight beyond Granny toward the ceiling. Great-Aunt Melissa was dead.

The doctor responded immediately to Granny's phone call, came to the house, pronounced Melissa dead, and arranged for the undertaker. He estimated that Melissa had died a little after 3:00 a.m.

*   *   *

Sarah refused to sleep upstairs for the rest of their visit, and Granny was happy to share her room. One week later, when the family returned to London, Granny went with them. She did not want to stay in Great-Aunt Melissa's house any longer either.

Chapter 4

The House

"Turn left at the light, Daddy," Sarah said, pointing with her right index finger. "The house is down that street about four blocks, and it's on the right." Ruby spun around in the front passenger seat to look quizzically at her daughter. Ken's attention was on the traffic. He seldom showed any interest in Sarah's predictions.

"How do you know, Sarah? You've never been to Windsor before." Her father had become cognizant of and accustomed to Sarah's unexplained foreknowledge. She seemed to "see" things more and more often lately. At first, Ken reacted much like Ruby; he denied and ignored as much and as long as he could but eventually had to acknowledge that his child had somehow developed extrasensory perception.

"I know, Dad, but I think I dreamed about the house last night. I can tell you what it looks like if you want me to," she suggested. Sarah was beginning to suspect that she was somehow being tested by her parents, and she wanted to prove to them that she just knew stuff sometimes. Ken smiled quickly in her direction without taking his eyes off the traffic, but his raised eyebrow told her that he accepted her offer.

"It's white wood with four windows on the front, two on each side of the little porch. You can't see in though 'cuz they have thick curtains. The house has no upstairs, and there is a carport on the right side of the house. The driveway is like the sidewalk, both made out of sidewalk stuff. You know what I mean, Dad?"

"Yes, honey, I know what you mean. They are made out of concrete."

"Yeah, that's it, concrete! They have a big yellow dog that sleeps in the doghouse in the backyard, and the yard has a high wood fence. Her name is Lacy, and she barks a lot, but she won't bite," Sarah explained. "Oh! And the front door is blue." Sarah did not like it when her parents doubted her, and she wanted to prove herself to them.

The family needed to buy a used washer and dryer because theirs was old, noisy, and undependable. Ken found an ad in the London daily newspaper, and they were now in Windsor, hoping to buy a new-to-them set. "That's the house, right there, Daddy," Sarah announced, and Ken parked the car next to the curb.

Ken matched the address painted on the curb to the address in the circled newspaper ad and was not at all surprised by his little girl's accuracy. "You should go into selling real estate when you get older," he teased. "This house is exactly as you advertised it!" Sarah's word picture painted for her father was now in empirical form, detail for detail, including the concrete driveway and sidewalk. Loud barks emanated from behind the tall wooden fence behind the house. "That must be Lacy," he teased as the four of them walked up the short sidewalk to the blue front door.

Suddenly Sarah stopped. "We can't go in there! Something bad is in there, Mom! We can't go in there!" She grabbed Ruby's hand and jerked hard on it. "Please, Mom! Don't make us go in there," she begged.

Ken and Ruby exchanged a hurried glance at each other, and then both focused on Sarah, who was trying to drag them back toward the street. She wanted them as far away from the little white house as fast as possible. Although still skeptical, Ruby and Ken allowed themselves to be pulled back to the car. James, wanting to get a peek at the dog, ran over to peer through a small opening in the backyard fence, but something blocked his view, so he turned back to the family as they returned to the car.

After the family's homeward journey was underway ten minutes, Ken turned to Sarah. "What was that all about, young lady? Why did we have to leave before we saw the washer and dryer? I hope they didn't see us. I'm a little embarrassed."

"They have a gun, Daddy, like a cowboy gun, on top of the fridge in the kitchen. I saw it!"

"We have never been there before. How could you see a gun?" Ken's patience with her obviously out-of-control imagination was wearing thin.

"I . . . I don't know," she stammered. "I just know!" She wanted to prove her story to her parents. "When you go in the back door, the kitchen has red roses on the walls and a brown floor like Mommy has in the bathroom. The fridge is beside the stove against the wall on the right, in front of the wood table and chairs. And the gun is on the top of the fridge. Why does the gun scare me, Daddy? I've never seen a real one, just on television."

"Sarah, you could not possibly have seen a gun. Besides, guns like that are illegal in Canada." Ken just wanted the conversation to end.

"What are you talking about, Sarah?" It was as if James suddenly became aware of the conversation. "What gun?"

"You don't know what we're talking about because you were over at the fence, James. What were you doing over there?" Ken was anxious to change the subject.

"I went to see the dog, but the men with the shovels were in the way," James explained. "There were three men, two had shovels, but the third one was sleeping on the ground."

Screech! The tires squealed as Ken slammed on the brakes and pulled over quickly into the roadside park. He turned to face James. "What do you mean, sleeping?" So James relayed his story again. Again, Ken and Ruby exchanged a hurried glance at each other, and then both focused on James.

"Oh my god!" Ken whispered in disbelief. "What were they doing with the shovels?" He actually hoped his little boy would laugh and say, "Just kidding!"

"Making a big hole."

Ken quickly located a payphone at the rest stop and called the police. He told them about the house, the address, why they were there, and what their little boy saw in the yard. He didn't tell them about his daughter or her sixth sense. If he needed to, he would but was reluctant because he didn't want the police to doubt his word. The officer on the other end of the line requested that Ken and his family return to the house but park a few houses away.

When they arrived, the police officers were already there, escorting two men in handcuffs out through the blue door. Ken told his family to stay in the car until he got back and went to speak with the policemen. After a brief introduction, the officer in charge thanked Ken for the tip and explained that they had found a deceased man, shot several times, beside a half-finished grave in the backyard. Something had interrupted their digging, and the two men had left the burial unfinished. The dead man's Detroit identification showed him to be an American citizen, and the police suspected he was involved in a border drug deal gone bad.

Ken listened to the officer intently. They had not yet found a weapon but were getting a search warrant. He hoped to find the gun somewhere in the house. Ken didn't tell him the gun was on top of the fridge. He really did not want to involve his young family any more than they were already. For now, he just thanked the officer. "Glad I could help," he said and quietly returned to his waiting family.

Thanks to his little girl, they were not harmed. He looked at Sarah as he got into the car. "You must be our guardian angel," he said and teasingly messed her hair. Sarah smiled. She was happy her father could see angels too.

CHAPTER 5

The Open Door

They were having one of Sarah's favourite things, a sleepover, and this pajama party was hosted at Shirley's house. The girls spent most of the evening doing normal, preteen-girl things: listening to the latest music on the radio, painting toenails and fingernails, braiding each other's hair, brushing teeth, and getting ready for bed. Now the girls were ready for the last part of their sleepover before turning in for the night. They excitedly planned to play with Shirley's new Ouija board.

"Does Jimmy love Carol?" Terri cautiously asked the Ouija board. Sarah and three of her twelve-year-old classmates, her best friends—Shirley, Carol, and Terri—all had their right index fingers cautiously on the pointer. They giggled with excitement as they sat circled on the bed in Shirley's dimly lit bedroom and waited for the pointer to move. Some girls at school had laughed at them for trying something so silly, but some said that they should not even consider messing with it. Some feared the board game was evil and would open the door to all kinds of bad things.

In unison, the girls shared one audible intake of breath as the pointer slowly moved to Yes. "Wow!" Carol said, and the others laughed. "It's my turn. Let me ask the next question."

"Okay, Carol," they all agreed.

"Does Joe love Sarah?" and the pointer moved slowly to No. Sarah then asked her question, if anyone else was in the room with them, and the pointer moved quickly to Yes.

Next it was Shirley's turn. "Who is here with us?" and the girls sat spellbound as the pointer spelled out M-e-l-i-s-s-a. Each suspected that one of them had been moving the pointer, but Carol, Shirley, and Terri didn't know anyone named Melissa. Only Sarah did, and she knew she hadn't moved the pointer. Besides, she had never forgotten the shaking bed incident and didn't want to ever hear from her great-aunt Melissa again.

"I think we should stop!" Sarah was visibly shaken. The others didn't know why because she had never shared about the night her great-aunt died. Sarah had not yet asked her question, but even in dim candlelight, they all saw the fear in Sarah's eyes. They all decided to move the pointer to Good-bye. That ended their first contact with the Ouija board.

                    *   *   *

Two weeks later, the girls met at Carol's house for another sleepover. Melissa's visit was a distant memory, and the girls were looking forward with anticipation to another game with the talking board as they chose to call it. They agreed ahead of time that their questions this time would not involve anyone other than the four of them.

Lights dimmed and candles lit, the girls were ready. Shirley asked her question first, "Will I be pretty when I grow up?" For a few seconds, nothing happened, but then the pointer began moving slowly to the Sun, indicating that conditions were favorable. Satisfied that she would be a pretty woman, Shirley turned to Carol for the next question.

"Will I have children?" and the pointer moved to Yes. Next, it was Terri's turn.

"Will I pass my English exam on Friday?" Again, the pointer moved to Yes. The three girls turned to Sarah, anxiously awaiting her question. They sensed her hesitation and feared that she would ask something she shouldn't.

"How many children will Carol have?" and the pointer moved to 3. They were enjoying the game so much, they forgot about their previous agreement to ask one question each and then stop.

Shirley wanted to know if she would have a handsome husband. Yes. Carol asked if she would pass the English exam. No. Terri questioned what her grade would be on the test, and the pointer moved first to 9 and then to 8. "Will I be pretty when I grow up?" Sarah asked, and the pointer moved very quickly to the Moon, indicating that, for her, conditions were unfavorable. At precisely the same moment, a silent voice audible only to Sarah, Great-Aunt Melissa's voice, whispered menacingly into Sarah's ear, "Ugly."

Sarah's eyes disappeared upward into her head as she rolled off her chair and onto the floor. She had fainted, bringing an immediate end to their second contact with the Ouija board. Carol ran to get a cold washcloth for Sarah's forehead while Shirley knelt, placing Sarah's head onto her lap, and Terri held her hand. The three concentrated on reviving Sarah, which took only a couple of minutes. When Sarah recovered sufficiently, she explained what had happened, and the girls vowed never to use the Ouija board again. Shirley put it back into the box, and the girls went to bed. Shirley, Terri, and Carol slept soundly the remainder of the night, but Sarah didn't sleep a wink. She lay on her back, eyes wide open, stared at the ceiling, and wondered why Great-Aunt Melissa was haunting her. She knew something was very wrong but couldn't identify it. Sarah only knew that she couldn't sleep.

What Sarah did not know was that by ending the session with the board without moving the pointer to Good-bye, the girls failed to close the door, to banish Melissa's spirit back to the land of the dead. They had inadvertently left the door to the underworld wide open.

*   *   *

The next morning, Ruby came to Shirley's house to pick up Sarah an hour earlier than planned. Ruby's eyes welled up and tears gushed like two mini waterfalls down her cheeks as she explained to Sarah that her granny had died in her sleep shortly after midnight.

Sarah immediately made the connection. She believed that Great-Aunt Melissa somehow caused Granny to die, and Sarah felt responsible; she blamed herself for opening the spirit door and allowing Melissa back into her life. This was the first time in Sarah's short life that someone she loved had died without giving her some sign or indication either before the death or at the time of her passing. It was too hard to explain it all to Mom, so Sarah kept it to herself.

*   *   *

The girls never played with the Ouija board again. The box was stored in Shirley's bedroom closet, and they never mentioned it. They did, however, continue to dabble with the occult. Buildings, churches, and graveyards said to be haunted peaked their collective interest.

The rumor at school was that the graveyard three blocks east of Shirley's house had several tombstones that glowed in the moonlight. It was close enough that the curious girls could easily ride their bicycles to the graveyard and be there within ten minutes. Nothing short of an edict from their parents could stop them from visiting the eerie place as soon as possible.

One week after releasing Melissa from the spirit hinterlands, the girls met at Sarah's house right after sundown and together headed to the graveyard, flashlights in hand, on their bicycles. The heavy iron gates sounded like a wounded animal howling in pain as the girls forced them open. "That was loud enough to wake the dead," Shirley teased as, in unison, they flicked on their flashlights and surveyed the various tombstones looking for an iridescent glow. They didn't have long to wait. The fifth stone directly in front of them, a large black granite stone with two gargoyles on top, glowed like fluorescent tubes were embedded deep within the rock.

"Wow!" they all said at once, and then exclamations followed rapidly. "Look at that!" "That's amazing!" "I've never seen anything like it!" "I wonder what makes it glow like that!" "Scary!" The girls were fascinated. "Wonder if there are any more like it?" For the next fifteen minutes the girls ran excitedly around the graveyard, looking for more glowing stones but didn't find any. Somewhat disappointed, they returned to the black gargoyle-crested stone, but when they shone their flashlights this time, the stone revealed no light whatsoever.

"What happened?" Shirley wanted to know, as did Carol and Terri. Sarah stood silent. A creeping suspicion crawled down her spine, tingling all the way to her toes, a suspicion that Great-Aunt Melissa was somehow involved.

"Let's go home," she said softly like she was afraid Melissa would hear her. "Let's go now!" louder this time, and the girls dashed to where they had left the iron gates open and found them closed. Overcome by terror, they didn't stop to open them again; instead, they all scampered up, over, and out of the graveyard as fast as they could, mounted their bicycles like cowboys mount saddled horses in old western movies, and headed back to the security of streetlight-lined streets. They pedaled silently and quickly all the way to Shirley's front yard. No one spoke. Without saying "Good night," Shirley hurried to her front door, and the others dispersed in separate directions heading to the safety of their individual homes.

*   *   *

The girls didn't even mention the word "haunted" for three weeks, but eventually, they craved more excitement; they had morphed into spirit-seeking junkies. They heard that the basement of the local Presbyterian church was haunted by several ghosts. Terri and Carol had attended youth group there for several years, so they were familiar with the building; they knew that a small basement window at the back of the building was never locked, and they could easily fit through the narrow opening.

Soon the girls found themselves breaking into the church. Terri and Carol went in through the window first, using boxes stacked behind the pastor's desk to facilitate their descent into the dense, dank blackness of the basement. They retrieved two taper candles from their shorts' pockets and lit them. Shirley and Sarah crawled in through the window and lit their candles too.

"Now what?" Sarah asked. "What should we do now?" as the four stood in the middle of the room. The girls gathered in the small roughly four-feet-wide circle of light cast by their candles. The weak candlelight failed to penetrate the intense blackness of the basement corners. "These candles are pretty much useless. They don't give enough light."

Suddenly, the girls were paralyzed by fear, a paralysis that lasted for less than thirty seconds. All four girls yelled, cried, pulled, clawed, and pushed each other out of the way as they all tried to exit through the small window at the same time. Later, beneath a streetlight, the girls reported hearing very different sounds. They had each heard a voice, and only one voice, although each described a different voice.

Carol heard a very soft, breathy female voice say "Hey!" Terri heard a young boy's voice say "Dude!" Shirley heard a woman's evil witch-like laughter, and Sarah heard Great-Aunt Melissa's grating, menacing voice scream "Get out!"

Chapter 6

Say Good-bye, Melissa

"How do we get rid of a ghost? Great-Aunt Melissa is terrifying me." Sarah told the others still in the soft streetlight glow about two blocks from the haunted church. "I mean it! We have to do something!" Her voice cracked with emotion as she fought back tears.

"My priest might know what we can do," Shirley offered. She heard Father Mitchell talking to her father about performing an exorcism several years before when he was in a different parish. "We can ask him. I don't think he'll laugh at us. That would be awful!"

They agreed to visit with Father Mitchell the following day after school. Shirley asked her dad, Mike Monroe, to invite the priest to their home about 4:00 p.m., and he made the arrangements. Shirley was very glad that her father didn't press her for details. She figured he would know soon enough and didn't want to relive it without the other girls there for moral support.

Father Mitchell arrived on time; he prided himself for always being punctual. He listened carefully as the girls relayed their strange tale of events—their first experience and the pointer spelling out Melissa's name, the second experience and Great-Aunt Melissa whispering "ugly" into Sarah's ear. Sarah explained about Great-Aunt Melissa dying, about the shaking bed, and about how she didn't like children. The priest seemed to listen more intently when they told of putting the board away without clicking on Good-bye.

Shirley's father sat spellbound as the girls each took a turn, telling what they heard in the basement of the church. His daughter had never exaggerated anything before, and he knew in his heart that she was telling the truth as she saw it.

"I think you girls left the door open between our world and the world of the dead. It is going to take some effort on your part, but you can undo the damage and send her spirit back to the other side," Father Mitchell explained. "I can give you some holy water and tell you what to do, but you will need to do the work yourselves. After all, you are the ones who invited Melissa into your world."

Father Mitchell instructed the girls to cut the Ouija board into seven pieces because the number 7 is believed to represent the fullness of God's love. "Seven is found over five hundred times in the Bible," he said. "Next, you must dig seven holes in seven different locations, place one piece of the board in each hole, and place a few drops of holy water onto each piece before burying it." He instructed them that it was the only way to effectively close the door and say good-bye to Great-Aunt Melissa once and for all.

Shirley's father agreed to help the girls perform the ritual the following day since it was Saturday. He drove them to seven locations to dispose of the pieces—the first was buried beneath the window of the Presbyterian church; the second at the base of the gargoyle-crested glowing tombstone; the third, fourth, fifth, and sixth pieces were buried in each of the girls' front yards; and the last one was buried at the gravesite of Shirley's mother. Her father thought that her mother, Mary Monroe, would still like to help her daughter even though she had crossed over nearly four years earlier.

When the last piece was covered, the girls looked at each other and smiled. They all sensed an inner peace they had not felt since first playing with the Ouija board.

CHAPTER 7

Premonitions

For the next six years, Sarah's life was relatively "spirit" less, except for a few notable occasions. Sarah was glad for the respite. The memory of Great-Aunt Melissa terrified her, and she never wanted to experience anything evil like that again.

The first occasion was when Sarah reached her fourteenth birthday. The snow lay almost five feet deep, wrapping her world in a fluffy, white, glittery blanket; it was cold but beautiful! Tommy, a sixteen-year-old boy from school, asked her to go snowmobile riding with him that afternoon, and she desperately wanted to go.

He was the cutest, most popular boy on campus because of his off-the-chart sense of humor. Although she was not quite old enough to date yet, she really liked Tommy and dearly loved snowmobiling. Nothing was more exciting than hearing the engine roar, feeling the wind tingle, nipping her rosy cheeks as the snowmobile raced across the open fields.

Something stopped her from going. She wasn't sure why, but when Tommy came to pick her up, she told him that she couldn't go. He pleaded with her. "Please, Sarah! You know how much you love snowmobiling, and your dad says you can go if you want to."

"Sorry, Tommy, something just doesn't feel right. I can't go." Her words contradicted what she really wanted to say. She couldn't believe she was telling him no.

Sarah watched him as he left. Tommy looked back over his shoulder. Puzzled by Sarah's rejection, he slowly climbed onto the snowmobile. Part of him hoped she would change her mind and come running out of the house, wearing her thick black-and-red snowsuit that made her look like the Michelin tire man, matching red hat, scarf, and gloves, and her Eskimo snow boots, ready for some fun. He loved the way she matched all her outfits; everything coordinated. That was the first thing he noticed about Sarah when he met her in Mr. Hildebrand's accounting class.

"Why didn't you go, Sarah?" her father questioned.

"I don't know, Dad. Something just doesn't feel right about it."

About four o'clock that afternoon, the phone rang, and Sarah answered. It was Shirley calling to tell her that Tommy was dead. "He was crossing from one farmer's field to another and didn't notice that the top wire of the fence was not buried in the snow. It cut off his head!" Sarah was speechless and in shock. She hung up without saying another word to Shirley.

At the funeral, as Sarah passed the casket, she wasn't surprised to hear Tommy's voice, audible only to her, whispering in her ear. *It's okay, Sarah. I'm glad you weren't with me when it happened.* Then he laughed. *Literally, I lost my head over you.* Only Tommy could find humor in a situation like this. Sarah couldn't help but smile. She felt that he was still with her somehow.

*   *   *

On another occasion, about six months later, Sarah dreamed that Shirley's house was on fire. She saw Shirley trapped in her bedroom with flames all around her. The dream was so vivid; Shirley was wearing purple-and-white pajamas, screaming as she huddled behind the bed in the corner, trying to avoid the roaring flames.

Sarah bolted out of bed, slipped into a housecoat, and ran barefoot out the back door. She didn't stop until she reached Shirley's house. The fire sirens grew in intensity as she neared it. The sidewalk's rough concrete tore at the soles of her feet, but Sarah didn't notice the blood. All she could think about was Shirley and prayed silently all the way as she ran.

When she got there, the first people Sarah saw were the fire emergency workers bringing Shirley out on a stretcher. She was wearing the purple-and-white pajamas Sarah had seen in the dream. Her long, brown hair was singed on the right side of her head, but otherwise, Shirley appeared unharmed.

"Thank God you're not burned!" Sarah blurted out as the firemen rolled the stretcher past her.

"Sarah! How did you know I was in a fire?" Then the surprise in Shirley's voice lessened. "Of course you knew. I forgot for a minute who I was talking to." Shirley secretly wished that she had Sarah's sixth sense and could see angels too.

"I saw it in a dream," Sarah called out to her as the ambulance doors closed.

*   *   *

Then, at age sixteen, Sarah went to the hospital to see her father's sister, Aunt Jane. Cancer's grey shadow hung over Jane's face as she lay on the hospital bed. Tubes seemed to be attached to every visible part of her frail, emaciated body. Her still-beautiful aquamarine eyes looked incongruent with the surrounding dark death circles that looked like a raccoon mask.

"Oh, Aunt Jane, how are you feeling? I hate to see you like this." Sarah loved her aunt Jane even though she didn't see her very often. Jane was always the life of the party at family get-togethers. Sarah fondly recalled every occasion—the backyard barbecues, swimming parties, birthday parties, and anniversaries.

"It's okay, honey. I can take it," but the shortness in Jane's breath exposed her cover-up. Sarah was not convinced. She knew Jane was truly suffering.

Sarah glanced over at the photograph of Jane's husband on the bedside table. Uncle Jack had been deceased for several years, but that unnerving black-and-white photograph was always with Jane wherever she went. The photograph bothered Sarah, but she didn't know why. Jack's eyes always seemed to follow her around the room. As she stood looking into Uncle Jack's piercing eyes, she distinctly heard his voice say "Soon." Sarah knew he was right.

She stood as though her feet were nailed to the cold, hard, ceramic-tiled hospital floor, not moving a muscle, and waited. About two hours later, Aunt Jane took her last breath. Sarah saw two angels take her out of the bed and out of the world, floating as they passed through the closed window. "Good-bye, Aunt Jane," she whispered softly. "I will always love you."

*   *   *

Sometimes Sarah hated her sixth sense, hated knowing when bad things were about to happen. She felt like she was having to live through them twice and wished she could be like her friends, oblivious and therefore disconnected until the actual event occurred. *Why me?* she wondered, and the image of the lady in red flashed through her mind.

Premonitions were not always negative. On rare occasions, Sarah had good news for her friends.

"So what should I do, Sarah? Should I go to the prom with Jimmy?" Carol asked as the four pajama-clad girls nestled on the overstuffed pink-and-purple brocade bedspread in Terri's room. "You know, a long time ago, the Ouija board said that Jimmy loved me. Do you remember?"

"I remember," Sarah responded. "Why are you asking me? You should do what you want to do, don't you think? Do you like him?"

"Yeah, I do. But, Sarah, I really respect your opinion. You know stuff, stuff that nobody else seems to know. You understand people better than anyone I know," Carol insisted. "So what should I do?"

"Okay," Sarah said, "if you insist." She crossed her legs and closed her eyes in a mimic-yoga pose. She sat quietly with her eyes shut for a couple of minutes as though waiting for an answer. When she opened her eyes, Carol was waiting for her answer. "Go to the prom with Jimmy. Carol, I think you two are going to be prom king and queen," and then she giggled.

"Really? Wow! That would be awesome! Why do you think that? How do you know?" Carol didn't want to get her hopes up if it wasn't a distinct possibility.

"I don't know how I know it, Carol. The thought just came to me, just now. It's like a voice told me." Sarah was not comfortable listening to the voice. She hadn't heard this particular voice since the lady in red visited when she was little and her mother asked her to not listen to the voice anymore. What if the voice was playing mind games with her? What if it was lying? The voice was familiar but still mostly untested.

"What about me?" Shirley asked. "Who should I go to prom with?" Sarah again closed her eyes and sat quietly. Shirley saw the tension appear in Sarah's posture, so she asked again, "Who should I go to prom with?"

Sarah didn't like to be pressured or where the conversation was going. "Shirley, I can't tell you who to date." Then she added, "Who has asked you to go with him?"

"Nobody, yet," Shirley admitted. Sarah told her to ask again when she had four or five possible dates for the dance, and both girls laughed. Terri told Shirley that, if nobody asked her, they could babysit together that night. They could rent a romantic movie and pop popcorn.

"So let's dye our hair! What do you think about some shade of auburn for all of us?" Terri asked. The girls giggled and busied themselves with mixing and applying the dye to each other's hair.

CHAPTER 8

Romance

"Hello," Sarah said when she picked up the phone. "This is Sarah."

"Sarah," the voice hesitated nervously. "This is Kevin Miller, the new boy in high school. Are you in Mrs. Brooks's first-period geometry class?"

Sarah smiled. She had noticed Kevin when he sat behind her in geometry class the day before and thought he was the most handsome guy she had ever seen—at least six feet tall, dark wavy hair, beautiful dark-brown eyes she could melt into, and an athletic build. "Yes, I am in Mrs. Brooks's first-period geometry class." She hoped that her voice sounded mature, like she was accustomed to talking with tall-dark-handsome callers, not the gushing, giddy, totally teen person hiding within her.

"Sarah, I know you don't know me, but would you consider going to the prom with me in two weeks?" He blurted it out quickly before he lost his nerve. "Or do you already have a date? I'm sorry. I should have asked that first. I'm sorry. A girl as beautiful as you probably has a date already. Heck, you probably have had a date for months already. I'm sorry. I gotta go. See you later," and he hung up, embarrassed by his own eagerness. Sarah stood speechless staring at the ring tone-humming phone in her hand for several minutes.

All Sarah had heard was that Kevin Miller thought she was beautiful! Sarah whispered to herself, "Wow! Kevin Miller thinks I'm beautiful!" For the next two hours, Sarah was on the phone with Shirley, Terri, and Carol. She wanted to tell them about the phone call, over and over again, so she could relive every word he said, not because her friends needed to hear it again and again. Kevin tried several times to call her back and apologize for hanging up on her but couldn't get through; the line was always busy.

*   *   *

The next morning, after an almost-sleepless night, Sarah got out of bed an hour earlier than usual. She wanted her hair and outfit to be absolutely perfect so she could have that I'm-this-beautiful-when-I-get-up-in-the-morning, all-natural look. She took one last glance at herself in the front foyer mirror as she left the house and was satisfied with her image. As usual, everything she wore was colour-coordinated—butterfly-rhinestone-embellished black jeans, pink sneakers, pink lacy camisole, and her black-and-pink sheer blouse. Her long flowing curls draped casually over her right shoulder like they found their current location totally by accident. *Okay. Let's do this,* she thought.

"Hope he talks to me today," Sarah told the girls when they met at the girls' locker bay before class. "Hope he asks me again. I want to go to prom with him so bad."

When the tardy bell rang and Kevin didn't come into the room, Sarah stopped staring at the door. Disappointed, she turned around and gave all her attention to Mrs. Brooks and the Pythagorean theorem. Sarah didn't notice when Kevin came late to class and slid into the desk behind her. "Wonder why he isn't here today," Sarah slid a note to Shirley. "I hope he isn't embarrassed about calling me."

Shirley read the note and smiled broadly. This was the first time anyone ever knew something before Sarah knew it, and Shirley was excited to be a part of it. Sarah saw the smile and knew immediately that Kevin was behind her. Her next note was for Kevin. "I would love to go to prom with you. Do you still want me to be your date?"

"You bet!" Kevin's response was immediate and loud. The class laughed; even Mrs. Brooks laughed. The attraction between Kevin and Sarah was obvious to everyone.

*   *   *

Kevin and Sarah became a couple from that moment on, a storybook romance. They were Romeo and Juliet without street fighting, family feuding, secret marrying, lying, and dying. They even looked perfect together, like bookends, like Barbie and Ken. Carol and Jimmy often double-dated with them; the four of them usually hung out together at most school events.

Shirley and Terri still hadn't met their Prince Charming; therefore, according to the unwritten teenage rules of dating for dummies, the girls made the ultimate friendship sacrifice and allowed Carol and Sarah to move on without them. In their minds, Carol and Sarah hadn't pulled away from them; instead, Shirley and Terri had willingly melted into the background, giving space for romance to blossom. The four girls were all still friends; they just weren't always together anymore.

From start to finish, prom was the ultimate experience, truly a night to remember, as it proclaimed in foil on the invitations and on the goblets. The guys picked the girls up in a white limousine. The hall's spectacular decorations—complete with candlelight, red-carpeted entrance way, vases filled with aromatic red roses, Grecian columns, mirrored glitter ball, lighted sheer-drapery-lined walls, chocolate fountain, punch fountain, and a functioning lighted waterfall—provided the perfect backdrop for the girls' beautiful formals and the guys' handsome rented black tuxedos.

Music was provided by a local band, the Country Cousins, a popular CKCO Channel 13 band from

Kitchener, Waterloo, and the four danced to almost every song, danced until their feet hurt, kicked off their shoes, and then danced some more. They wanted to enjoy every second.

The highlight of the evening occurred when the announcer said that prom king and queen were Carol and Jimmy. Carol smiled knowingly in Sarah's direction, but Sarah didn't smile back. She didn't want Kevin to know about her extrasensory perception, not yet.

CHAPTER 9

Kevin Learns about Sarah's ESP

"I have heard a lot about Sammy's Pizza," Sarah told Kevin when he picked her up in his red 1978 Ford Mustang. "It's supposed to be the best pizza in town." They planned to meet Carol and Jimmy at the restaurant for a double date—pizza followed by a movie.

When they pulled up to the curb, Sarah could see the owner through the small store's over sized front bay window; Sarah watched as the owner, Sammy, tossed what looked like a baseball-sized lump of pizza dough into the air. His dexterity fascinated her as the small lump of dough transformed into a large, thin pizza base. The dough spun continuously round and round as it soared up and down several times; each time, Sammy skillfully caught it, tossing it up again without breaking the dough. She had never seen anything like it before.

"How does he do that? Look at him, Kevin. That dough looks like a flying saucer! What keeps it from breaking?" Sarah wanted to watch Sammy make more pizzas, but Carol and Jimmy caught her attention when they pulled up next to Kevin's car. She called out to them, "Let's go in and get a table near the front. I want to watch that guy make another one. You should have seen it, Carol," and hurried to the glass front door. The others were not far behind.

The inside of the restaurant could have been called Little Italy. Sarah felt like she had been magically transported across the globe into another culture. Romantic Italian music floated around the candlelit room. Tapers, held by multicoloured wax-encrusted empty wine bottles, burned on every table. Mural-sized photos of vineyards lined the walls. Romantic ambiance blended softly with the enticing pizza-baking aroma.

The front of the store was a bustle of activity. In addition to Sammy busily tossing pizza dough, another man piled toppings onto the dough in an assembly-line fashion. Still another took the cooked pizzas out of the huge oven and boxed them for delivery. A steady stream of delivery drivers filed in, carrying empty insulated pizza carriers, and out again, carrying stacks of pizza-box-stuffed carriers. A pretty brunette woman finished taking an order over the telephone and guided the four customers to a bistro-style table close to the front. Kevin and Jimmy pulled the girls' chairs out for them as the hostess placed four menus on the table and left to answer the phone.

"This is such a romantic place," Carol said after the boys seated themselves. "Thanks for bringing us here, guys."

"Doesn't the pizza smell great, Kevin?" Jimmy asked. "What kind of pizza should we order? Girls, do you two have a favourite?"

"Carol and I both like ham and pineapple," Sarah replied, "but we can eat whatever you guys want. Is that okay, Carol?"

"You bet." The girls chose their beverages and added, "Guys, do you mind if we go to the restroom first?" They wanted to check their makeup.

"Not at all," both guys said almost in unison, and the girls left in search of the restroom.

"Isn't this a cute place, Carol?" Sarah said as she applied a fresh coat of her favourite cherry-red lipstick. "Even the restroom is romantic." She giggled.

"Sure is." Carol ran a comb through her long curly locks. "Say, Sarah, I have been meaning to ask you something. Have you told Kevin about your ESP yet? I think you should tell him before somebody else mentions it."

"Not yet, Carol. I am a little afraid to because I don't know how he'll react. Some people think that kind of stuff is just creepy." They took one more look at themselves and then, satisfied that they looked beautiful, returned to the table.

During the girls' absence, the mood at the table changed from romantic and jovial to quiet and reserved. Kevin didn't say more than ten words during the whole meal. Sarah and Carol assumed that the guys had disagreed about something, so they never mentioned the change, and everyone ate in awkward silence. After the guys paid their bill, they all headed to the movie. Kevin and Sarah still had not talked much.

"What's wrong, Kevin?" she finally asked. "You have been really quiet. Did I do something that upset you?"

Kevin pulled over to the curb and turned to face her. He didn't want to have this conversation while driving; he wanted to give her all his attention. "Sarah, I heard what you said in the restroom. The walls in there must be as thin as cardboard. What do you mean, ESP? Are you psychic? Because I don't believe in that kind of voodoo creepy stuff."

Sarah's heart sank. *How can I possibly explain my ESP to Kevin if he thinks it's creepy?* Sarah thought. *I need to choose my words very carefully.*

The pregnant pause between them was almost palpable. Finally she spoke, "Kevin, I don't know how to tell you, but whether you believe in ESP or not, I seem to have extrasensory perception." She told him everything that had happened, from the lady in red when she was only eight years old to knowing that Carol and Jimmy would be chosen king and queen at the prom over a month before. Kevin listened carefully. His skepticism weakened incrementally with each incident; the events that really got his attention were Tommy's snowmobile accident and the fire at Shirley's house. In the final analysis, Kevin became a still-skeptical pseudo believer.

"Sarah, if you believe you have ESP, and it sure sounds like you have something, then I guess you probably do." Kevin couldn't believe what he was saying, but it made Sarah smile, so he was glad he said it. "Sarah, I knew you were special. Guess I didn't realise just how totally special you really are." He leaned over and kissed her, turned on the motor, and headed back into the traffic. "Thank you for telling me, Sarah. I know it must have been hard for you to do that. Let's go to the movie," he smiled at her. "Carol and Jimmy must think we got lost."

CHAPTER 10

Police and Doughnuts

About a month later, Kevin picked Sarah up for school an hour earlier than usual. "Let's go to Tim Hortons and grab a couple of doughnuts before class. Okay?" he asked, and Sarah readily agreed. Sarah loved their oh-so-special doughnuts; she thought they must be the best in the world, maybe even the universe.

"They sure are busy this morning, Sarah. Look at the line of people in there. We'll have to wait a bit. Is that okay?"

Sarah's eyes focused on the people. She grew silent, like she was imitating the *Thinker* again. Suddenly she broke her silence, and her voice sounded urgent. "We can't go in there, Kevin!" She had to make Kevin listen to her even though nothing appeared to be out of the ordinary in the doughnut shop. They were always busy in there. After all, they made the very best doughnuts.

"Why not, Sarah?" Kevin's confusion was obvious. Sarah had been so anxious for doughnuts just a few minutes before.

"Kevin, call 911! Tim Hortons doughnut shop is about to be robbed. The last two guys in that line have guns under their shirts."

"What? How do you know that? I don't see any guns." Then he remembered her ESP. "Is this one of those premonition things you told me about?" and his inner skeptic overpowered his believer. He thought, *She must be a little crazy.*

Sarah hadn't taken her eyes off the two men in the line. She was trying to memorize their appearance just in case they got away. She noted that both were about five and a half feet tall, probably in their twenties, dark-haired, and slightly overweight. Both men wore blue jeans and coloured T-shirts—one was blue, the other one white. Without hesitation, she insisted, "Kevin, call 911. Hurry! I am so scared somebody is going to be hurt. Please hurry. Make the call."

"Okay. I'll do it, but they're going to think I'm crazy. How can you report a robbery before it happens?" Even though he thought that he must be out of his mind, Kevin hesitantly dialed the number. "Hello. Um, this is Kevin Miller. I am reporting a robbery in progress at Tim Hortons doughnut shop on Dundas Street. There are two men in there that have guns." He listened for a few seconds and added, "Yes. That is correct. Please hurry."

Kevin and Sarah stayed in the car, watching the two men inside. Only two minutes passed, and the police were on scene. "Oh no, Sarah," he sounded really upset. "The guys haven't done anything, and the cops are here. Now what do we do? We'll look so stupid!" and he started his engine. "We gotta get outta here," but before he could put the transmission in reverse, the two inside made their move, and so did the police.

The robbers pulled their guns. One man pointed his at the startled young woman behind the counter; the other man ordered everyone to put all their money and valuables into a paper bag. At the same moment, two police officers approached from behind them, pointed their guns at the robbers, and ordered them to drop their weapons. Within fifteen seconds, the robbery began and ended. The policemen were proud of themselves. Nobody was robbed. Nobody was harmed. As Kevin watched, the two robbers were handcuffed and placed in the backseat of the police car, and the two policemen were rewarded with a couple of free doughnuts.

Kevin sat transfixed, staring into the doughnut shop. His eyes grew wide, and his lower jaw seemed unattached to the rest of his face. *Sarah was right! She really does have ESP,* he thought, *Totally awesome!* Then aloud, he said, "Sarah, I can't believe what just happened! How did you know? Wow! I am so impressed with you right now."

The police officers and 911 operator never connected the timeline of events; the robbery was reported at least two minutes before it actually happened. "All's well that ends well," Kevin smiled at Sarah. "No harm, no foul. I think I love you, you crazy lady." Believer Kevin overpowered Skeptic Kevin at that moment. Pseudo believer morphed into a full-fledged believer. He thought to himself, *I must be the only guy in town lucky enough to have an awesome, oh-so-special girlfriend.*

CHAPTER 11

Plans

The next few months passed without any unexplainable incidents. Kevin and Sarah both celebrated graduation from grade twelve. Kevin applied to the University of Waterloo because he wanted to pursue his career choice, becoming a medical doctor. However, his application was denied. The university required all premed students to have an additional year of high school, grade thirteen, essentially the freshman year of college available for Canadian students at the high school level. Reluctantly, Kevin enrolled in grade thirteen.

The evening before his first day of class, Kevin surprised Sarah with another trip to Sammy's Pizza followed by a movie, essentially a do-over date of the one they had once shared with Jimmy and Carol. Kevin even pulled over to the curb at the same place he had stopped months earlier because he wanted to talk to Sarah. This time he had a different topic on his mind.

"Sarah, I have been crazy about you ever since the first time I saw you in geometry class," he said as he turned to face her. Nervously, Kevin slid his shaking hand into his khaki windbreaker jacket pocket and retrieved a small velvet-covered navy-blue ring box. Kevin wanted to look straight into her eyes as he added, "Will you marry me? I know I don't have much to offer you right now. I'm still basically a high school student, but I promise that I will take care of you. It won't be long before I'll be in college, then medical school, then interning somewhere. Honey, would you consider becoming Mrs. Dr. Kevin Miller? We can be married as soon as I finish grade thirteen. Do you believe in long engagements? Sarah, please say yes."

Sarah thought he would never stop talking. She hadn't really heard or understood anything he said after his first four words, "Will you marry me?" "Yes," she whispered, but he didn't hear her and kept talking.

"Honey, if you want to think about it for a while, I'll wait for your answer. You can tell me in a month or two. It's okay. I know I shouldn't be so pushy, but I just can't help myself. I'm sorry that—"

"Yes!" she repeated, louder this time, and Kevin finally stopped talking.

"What did you say?" He couldn't believe his ears. "Did you say yes?"

"Of course, I'll marry you," and a flood of I-am-so-happy-I-can't-stand-it tears flowed down her cheeks like mini waterfalls. Kevin slipped a small five-point solitaire diamond ring onto Sarah's left hand. She thought it must be the largest diamond she had ever seen.

*   *   *

Sarah put her own college plans on hold for a few years so she could help Kevin start his. She thought his career was more important since he would be the primary wage earner. Sarah got a job working as counter staff at Tim Hortons, the same place where her ESP prevented the robbery, because she wanted to help pay for their upcoming wedding. Kevin found a part-time evening job delivering for Sammy's Pizza. Whenever the couple had any time off work, they were together, inseparable.

Sarah dreaded the inevitable, meeting Kevin's family. She put it off as long as she could but finally ran out of excuses. His father's job was transferring them to Stratford. Kevin was anxious for them to meet his fiancée, the love of his life, but first he had to find a place for him to live so he could stay close to Sarah.

He moved into Jimmy's unattached, two-car garage, which had been converted into a small but comfortable apartment. Jimmy and his father renovated it by first removing the double overhead door and replacing it with a cinder-block wall containing a bright-red decorative house door and a double-paned window. The bare-bulb ceiling light was replaced with a decorative four-light ceiling fan. A roomy closet was built into the back left corner of the room. Insulation and carpeting were then added, and the walls were painted white. Next, they installed a safety door in the back wall. In the back right corner, a small room containing a shower stall, commode, and sink finished Kevin's new home.

His new pad, as Kevin preferred to call it, was big enough to accommodate all his possessions—a single bed, dresser, chest of drawers, folding card table, two chairs, small television, and an almost-new brown imitation-leather-covered settee he found at the Salvation Army store for ten dollars. Jimmy provided him with a space heater for winter and a fan for the summer months. What made it home for Kevin was a framed eight-by-ten photo of Sarah and him at the prom. He placed it next to his bed so it would be the last thing he looked at before he fell asleep each night and the first thing when he opened his eyes in the morning.

* * *

"Sarah, this is my mom and dad," Kevin held the door open for Sarah. He knew how nervous she was and hoped that his parents would love her as much as he did.

"We have heard so much about you, we feel like we already know you." Kevin's parents greeted Sarah warmly. "We are excited to finally meet you."

Sarah blushed. She could feel her face turning red. "Thank you," she replied, and the softness in her own voice surprised her. "Kevin has told me a lot about you too." Sarah offered her right hand in greeting, but his mother gently brushed it aside and hugged her. Sarah liked her immediately and felt a little less anxious.

"I'm Gloria, and I know we are going to be good friends." The tall, slender, smiling lady standing in front of her reminded Sarah of someone she met before, but she couldn't remember where. Sarah thought the woman must be the most beautiful middle-aged woman she ever met. The woman's wide smile was immediately comforting, and Sarah wondered why she had expected Kevin's mother to be a much-older woman. Her dark wavy shoulder-length hair glistened like a doll's acrylic hairdo, reflecting the lights of the crystal chandelier in the next room. "My goodness, what has my son been telling you about me?"

"Just that you teach grade three, and your students love you," Sarah smiled. Then turning her attention to

Kevin's father, she once again offered her hand. "You must be Jim." She thought to herself that even though Jim was slightly balding, he was almost as handsome as Kevin. He was not at all the stereotypical certified public accountant she had expected.

Jim shook her hand firmly and, still shaking it, turned to Kevin. "You're right, son. She really is a beauty. Guess we both know how to pick 'em, eh?" Everyone laughed and tensions disappeared as quickly as vaporized steam. "Gloria, let's all go sit in the living room. It's a lot more comfortable there than standing here in the foyer. What are we having for supper? It sure does smell good!"

Sarah wondered why she had ever been nervous about meeting Kevin's family. She already felt like she was part of the family.

*   *   *

One week later, Kevin and Sarah both helped Jim and Gloria box up their household belongings in preparation for the movers. Jim was being reassigned to the Stratford branch of his CPA firm, and Gloria felt fortunate to find another grade-three teaching position even though the school year was well underway. She would take over for the previous teacher, who had to leave unexpectedly because of family problems.

"Where do you and Kevin plan to be married," Gloria asked as she carefully wrapped the last drinking glass in the kitchen cabinet. "Would you consider being married in Stratford?" She paused briefly and added, "We really hope you will agree to marry where Jim and I plan to attend church. That way, we can be more involved in planning it."

"I . . . I don't know what to say." Sarah didn't want to make any decisions about anything without first talking it over with Kevin. "Have you asked Kevin yet?" She thought about it for a couple of minutes and then added, "Can we give you an answer in a couple of months? We don't plan to marry until he finishes grade thirteen, so we have plenty of time." Gloria agreed, and the subject was dropped.

Sarah finished helping Gloria box up the last of her dishes and stacked the boxes in the garage. The movers would be there early the next morning, and Sarah felt secretly relieved that Gloria would not be around every day. Even though she already felt bonded with her future mother-in-law, something troubled her; Sarah wished she could remember where she might have met Gloria before.

CHAPTER 12

I Do

The school year flew by in a whirlwind of activity. Kevin studied hard and earned top grades, ensuring acceptance into University of Waterloo's premed program. Even though Ruby and Ken offered to shoulder most of the wedding's financial burden, both Sarah and Kevin worked every day and saved as much as they could in anticipation of their upcoming wedding.

The couple planned to be married on June 1 in Gloria and Jim's new church in Stratford, at the recently renovated United Church. Sarah wanted all her friends to be a part of the ceremony, and everyone eagerly accepted. James agreed to participate as best man, Carol as maid of honor, Jimmy as usher, and Shirley and Terri as bridesmaids. Of course, Ruby and Ken would be assigned seats across the aisle from Gloria and Jim in the front row. No negative premonitions or spiritual visitations interrupted Sarah's euphoria. It was as though the entire universe was perfectly aligned to produce the perfect wedding for Sarah and Kevin. Sarah had always dreamed of being a June bride.

Invitations were sent out to literally hundreds of family members and friends. Dresses and suits were purchased and fitted, flowers were chosen and ordered, rings were selected and purchased, and church decorations were stored and ready to be placed in the sanctuary. All their friends and relatives RSVP'd, so the couple expected the church to be full. Even the weather forecaster predicted a warm, sunny day.

*   *   *

Carol, Shirley, and Terri looked Barbie-doll beautiful in their floor-length spaghetti-strapped cranberry-red dresses that were fitted to the waist and flowed gracefully to just above their matching stiletto heels. All three busily hovered around Sarah, adjusting her sequined-and-pearled strapless bridal gown and veil and carefully applying the finishing touches to her makeup.

"Sarah, we are all so happy for you and Kevin," Carol almost cried as she spoke. "You two are perfect together. You make us believe true love really does exist!" Carol wanted to tell Sarah that Jimmy proposed to her the night before but chose not to tell her, not yet anyway. She didn't want to detract any attention away from Sarah on her very special day. Today, Carol wanted everyone's thoughts on Sarah and Kevin. "I sure will miss you two when you move to Waterloo," she added.

"The church is packed, Sarah! I snuck a peek a few minutes ago," Terri excitedly gushed. "Gosh, Kevin's family must be huge. Sure are a lot of people I've never seen before."

"That's perfect!" Shirley said as she gently arranged Sarah's flowing veil and handed her the bridal bouquet of red roses and delicate white baby's breath. "Carol, should I go tell the minister we are ready?" Carol nodded and Shirley hurried into the minister's study to deliver the message.

Sarah's father was waiting patiently by the sanctuary entrance to escort his daughter when the girls arrived to take their assigned places, ready for the longest short journey down the aisle. An extremely nervous bridegroom waited with James and the minister by the altar at the front of the church. Although Sarah couldn't see the organist, somehow the organist knew she was ready and immediately began playing the wedding march. Carol, Shirley, and Terri led the procession. Ken whispered, "Sarah, you look beautiful. Kevin is one lucky guy!"

Sarah felt her cheeks blush as she quietly responded, "Thank you, Dad." At that moment, nothing else mattered. Her eyes were on Kevin who was now glancing at her over his shoulder in anticipation.

As though the ceremony had been recorded and was being played on a broken tape, only snippets of the minister's words actually reached either Sarah's or Kevin's ears. They were lost in each other's eyes; the audience faded into the background, became white noise. "We are gathered here . . . Do you take this man . . . to love and to cherish . . . 'til death do you part?" In unison, the congregation inhaled as they waited for Sarah's answer. She didn't respond.

Kevin suppressed a grin. He knew his beautiful bride was focused on him and not really listening to the preacher. "Sarah, it's your turn to speak," Kevin whispered, and everyone smiled and held their collective breath.

"Oh, I do!" Sarah blushed, and everyone giggled and exhaled, sounding similar to a bicycle tire suddenly losing its air.

Then the preacher's monotone voice continued, "Do you take this woman . . . in sickness and health . . . 'til death do you part?" and Kevin quickly and loudly responded, "I do." Like they were still in geometry class, the attraction between Kevin and Sarah was obvious to everyone. Kevin didn't wait for the minister's permission to kiss his bride; he gently held her close and kissed her tenderly, passionately, scintillatingly, hotly.

"Ladies and gentlemen, it is my pleasure to present to you Mr. and Mrs. Kevin Miller." To Kevin and Sarah, no one else was in the room, only they existed—not the preacher, organist, family members, or friends—not even the attractive brunette lady wearing a bright red dress seated in the front row next to Gloria and Jim.

CHAPTER 13

Special Delivery

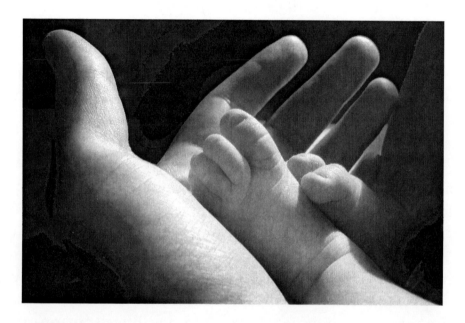

The couple rented a small, affordable, two-bedroom, one-bath, fully furnished upstairs apartment, which was actually converted attic space, within walking distance to the university. The apartment was totally sequestered with a private street-level bright-red entrance separate from the main-floor apartment. The stairs leading up to their floor reminded Sarah of the narrow stairway at Great-Aunt Melissa's house.

Although the apartment offered limited space, the landlord had incorporated every square inch of available floor space. Sarah loved the small kitchen, which connected to the master bedroom which connected to the bathroom. One end of the kitchen opened up into a small hallway, which connected to the long, very narrow, windowless living room which connected to the smaller bedroom. What the apartment lacked in architectural flow, it compensated for in what Sarah called cuteness. "The apartment is absolutely perfect, a wonderful first home for us," she told Kevin. In fact, all the apartment lacked was adequate closet space; the master bedroom contained one small closet, and the hall contained an oddly incongruous, floor-level, three-feet-high by six-feet-long closet with one shelf that could be used to store out-of-season clothing, shoes, and winter boots. Sarah and Kevin didn't notice that only the bedrooms had windows. Most of their home time was spent looking at each other anyway, so the view outside didn't concern them.

Sarah found a job selling women's shoes at a nearby Sears Department Store, and Kevin officially began his classes at University of Waterloo. Together, they transformed the small bedroom into a study for Kevin. Sarah discovered a new talent, cooking, and anxiously hurried home after work each day to experiment with some of Ruby's and Gloria's recipes. Sarah often teased Kevin that she could feed him toasted cardboard, and he would think it was delicious just because she made it for him.

Then the by-now-familiar, discomforting sense of a paranormal presence began surfacing back into Sarah's consciousness. She was standing at the kitchen sink, washing breakfast dishes one morning, when she felt a sudden icy chill like a spirit just passed behind her. It disappeared as quickly as it began, but the scent of Old Spice men's cologne floated through the room. It started with just a suggestion of the scent, grew into a stifling intensity, and faded away as quickly as it began. "That's very strange," Sarah said aloud. "Where on earth did that smell come from?" Her father was the only man she knew that used Old Spice. She told Kevin about the scent that evening during supper, and he assured her that it must have somehow floated up through the kitchen pipes from the apartment below. She accepted Kevin's reasoning and privately scolded herself for her overactive imagination.

About two months later, Sarah came home from work early because she didn't feel well. As she came up the stairwell, she felt a sudden blast of very cold air and decided that she should lie down for a while. *I must have a fever,* she thought and curled up under a quilt on top of the bed. Sarah clung tightly to her pillow and mattress as the room swirled like a wild roller coaster, just as it had done when she was a very ill eight-year-old. She felt herself falling helplessly as a wave of nausea enveloped her, and she dashed into the bathroom. Clinging tightly to the commode into which she involuntarily emptied her stomach contents, Sarah became aware of a sound coming from the bedroom closet. It sounded like wire clothes hangers rattling; she struggled to stop retching and concentrated on identifying the sound. *I know I'm not imagining that noise,* she thought and opened the closet door to investigate as soon as the floor stopped whirling. She found nothing unusual; their meticulously ironed clothes hung unwrinkled and evenly spaced on the single wooden dowel rod. No hangers were disturbed; it was exactly as she had left it that morning. Exhausted and still feeling nauseated, Sarah lay back down and drifted into a peaceful, undisturbed two-hour nap from which she woke up refreshed, feeling well once again.

The following morning, Sarah again had to come home early. Once again, her nausea was overwhelming, although brief. When Kevin came home from classes that evening, arms loaded with anatomy and physiology books, he was surprised to find Sarah unusually pensive. "What's the matter, sweetheart? You don't look like yourself tonight," Kevin asked. "Are you not feeling well again?"

"I'm okay now, but I had to come home early again today because I was throwing up," Sarah sobbed. "If I keep on getting sick, I'm afraid they'll fire me."

"You've been sick two days in a row," Kevin said softly speaking more to him than to Sarah. "Honey, I'm still a long way from being a doctor, but I think you may be pregnant. I love you and don't care if you work or not. So what if they fire you?" The next day, Sarah confirmed Kevin's suspicions when she took a home pregnancy test, and together they made an appointment with Dr. Campbell, an ob-gyn at the Kitchener-Waterloo Clinic.

Sarah's morning sickness continued every day for the following four weeks, but she was not fired from her job. Her boss was the mother of five children, so she knew and understood Sarah's situation very well.

During Sarah's second trimester, paranormal activity in her home began to occur more often. Kevin and Sarah always made sure their street-level door stayed locked, especially before going to bed. However, on several occasions, they awoke in the morning to find the door unlocked and slightly ajar. The first time it happened, they quietly accused each other. When it continued to happen, both suspected they had an uninvited house guest; maybe a former tenant still had a key, or the landlord felt a need to open the door and absentmindedly left it open. As though talking about it would exacerbate the problem, neither wanted to discuss it. The problem of the occasionally unlocked door soon became dwarfed by other more-pressing unexplained events.

One evening, snuggling on the couch, watching a movie on their small television, Sarah and Kevin were startled by the unmistakable sound of silverware rattling in the kitchen. "Stay here, honey." Kevin whispered "Someone is in the kitchen" and raised his index finger to his lips signaling that she should not make a sound. Both thought immediately of their mysterious, occasionally unlocked front door and wished they had simply replaced the obviously defective lock. Sarah waited, expecting to hear a commotion as Kevin confronted the intruder, but she heard nothing. "Sarah, come into the kitchen for a minute. I want you to see this." Kevin's voice indicated his confusion.

"What is it?" Sarah hesitated at the kitchen/hall doorway. "What's going on?"

"Nothing," he responded, "absolutely nothing. I found nothing. The silverware drawer is closed, and all our silverware is in the—" Before he could finish his sentence, they both heard the sound of water running in the bathroom. "What the devil?" Kevin said and headed to the bathroom expecting to find an intruder. Again, he found nothing. The sink was dry. Obviously, there was no water running. Kevin and Sarah stood speechless, puzzled for a couple of minutes and stayed speechless as they returned to the living room. Both stopped suddenly at the living room entrance. The neat, organized room they had left minutes before was now a mess. Magazines that were stacked on the coffee table were strewn on the floor; throw cushions from the couch were at the other end of the long, narrow room. "Oh my god," Kevin announced. "What is going on?"

Sarah struggled to assure him that somehow the unexplainable could be explained. By now, she believed beyond any doubt that her home was haunted, probably by a poltergeist, a spirit being powerful enough to toss things around in the physical world. However, not wanting to upset Kevin any more than he already was, she offered an explanation he could accept. "Honey, you know that it's Halloween tonight. Some kids were just playing a trick on us, don't you think?" Then she stated the obvious, "Honey, we need to get a better lock on that door!"

Kevin changed the lock the following day, and life returned to normal. They experienced no more Old Spice aroma, rattling silverware, disheveled living room, running water, or unlocked doors—for almost two months. The night before Christmas, as they enjoyed their first Christmas tree—a spindly, sparsely decorated Charlie Brown-style Christmas tree—the kitchen light suddenly flickered on and off several times. Kevin went to investigate; he checked the wall switch and the fuse box but found no problem with either, so he returned to the living room. The kitchen remained unlit for the remainder of the evening, but at midnight, when the couple had been asleep for two hours, the lights began flickering again. "That's just crazy," he told Sarah. "We won't be able to get an electrician up here until after Boxing Day, so guess we'll just have to put up with it until then. Let's just ignore it for now, and I'll have it fixed soon as I can. Go back to sleep, sweetheart," and he kissed her gently on the forehead. "Tomorrow is a big day."

*   *   *

Like an overstuffed Christmas stocking, their tiny apartment was literally stuffed with people; Gloria, Jim, Ruby, Ken, and James celebrated the day with Kevin and Sarah. Gloria and Ruby prepared and brought most of the meal with them, and Sarah was grateful for their contributions. Since she was entering her third trimester, her tiny baby bump was expanding, and she was easily fatigued. Insomnia often kept her from enjoying a full night's sleep lately. Sarah excitedly took enough photographs with the new Polaroid camera Gloria gave her for Christmas to fill two family albums. Everybody enjoyed the day. The meal was perfect. Nobody seemed to mind the cramped conditions. Sarah and Kevin's first Christmas as husband and wife was the best they ever had.

Since the next day was Boxing Day, they both had the day off, giving them some quiet time to just relax. Sarah brought out the photographs from the day before and laid them out on the kitchen table as Kevin ate his breakfast. Sarah still had a little trouble keeping food down, so she settled for just a cup of coffee and a slice of dry toast.

"Look at this one of your mom, Kevin. She looks so pretty. I loved her Christmas blouse, didn't you?" Not waiting for him to answer because she just wanted to enjoy the day all over again through the photos, Sarah continued. "Oh, honey, look at this one of Jimmy. He's growing up to be so handsome, don't you think?"

Suddenly, she stopped talking. When Kevin looked up, the startled look on her face frightened him a little. "Hon, what's wrong?"

"Look at this picture," she said. "Do you see anything strange in it?" Sarah held the photo up so Kevin could see it better. "Look in the bottom right corner. What do you see?"

Kevin's lower jaw dropped uncontrollably. He couldn't believe his eyes. "Babe, is that a little girl? Who is it?" The slightly out-of-focus image of a child, maybe as young as four years old, was clearly peeking around the corner. Her long dark hair contrasted with her white dress. "This is unbelievable!" Kevin sat silent for a minute and then added, "Do you suppose she was messing with our lights? That would certainly explain things, eh?" Kevin knew that life with his psychic Sarah was going to be interesting, but he had no idea how interesting it would become.

* * *

Sarah was glad that the following eleven weeks passed quickly with nothing unusual happening. Her psychic abilities told her that her baby boy would have all of Kevin's handsome features, his dark hair and eyes. Kevin found a reasonably priced small chest of drawers at the Salvation Army for the baby's clothes. Every day, Sarah excitedly unfolded and refolded every piece of the baby's clothing, picturing her son wearing them. They received a stroller, crib, high chair, and car seat from family and friends who gave Sarah a baby shower. Sarah had been buying disposable diapers for months and storing them in the odd hall closet. She was ready.

*   *   *

In the middle of the worst snowstorm of the year, at two o'clock in the morning, the baby was ready too. Sarah's first contractions began in earnest, surprising her by their intensity. She had expected the onset of labor to begin gently and build slowly, but Kevin timed her first contractions at only three minutes apart. He had to get her to the hospital, fast!

He grabbed her small overnight suitcase and was helping her get to the car. About halfway down the stairs, another contraction seized Sarah, causing her to buckle over in severe pain. She lost her footing and fell the last six stairs, striking her head on the railing and landing hard against the red door.

"Oh my god!" Kevin looked at his unresponsive wife curled up in the fetal position at the base of the stairs, blood trickling down the side of her head. "Sarah, it's going to be okay! I'm calling 911 right now. Hold on, baby!" Kevin made an urgent call for help, and help arrived in just two minutes. Since the roads were snow covered and icy, their fast response surprised Kevin. In less than five minutes after calling, Sarah was once again conscious, head bandaged, still in intense labor, in the ambulance, and on her way to the hospital.

She was taken immediately to the delivery room. Dr. Campbell examined her and looked very serious as he listened for a fetal heartbeat. The baby was coming and coming fast but in breach. His little legs were already in the birth canal, so a Caesarean delivery was not an option. The baby might not survive if the umbilical cord should wrap itself around his neck during delivery. Because of Sarah's serious condition, Kevin was not permitted in the delivery room; he was taken to the waiting room down the hall and was not allowed to help the love of his life fight the biggest battle of her life.

But Sarah wasn't alone. The doctor and several nurses were in the room, but Sarah was unaware of them. She had somehow entered another dimension, one without contractions. Sarah was pleased to see she had visitors—Granny, Aunt Jane, Uncle Jack, and even Tommy, the boy from school. They were sitting on a bench against the wall. "Don't be afraid, Sarah. You are going to be okay," Granny said and the others nodded in agreement. "Your beautiful baby boy is going to be okay too," she added. Suddenly Sarah was jolted back into reality by the worst pain she could have ever imagined. Her visitors were gone, and she could see the top of the doctor's head as he worked feverishly behind the white sheet. Just as suddenly as the contractions began, they stopped, and Sarah heard the soft, tender cry of her newborn son.

*   *   *

Kevin stood speechless when the doctor came out of the delivery room. "Congratulations, Mr. Miller, it's a boy," the doctor said, "and he has ten fingers and ten toes. He's beautiful, and your courageous wife is doing fine. She is sedated, and we will keep her in recovery for a couple of hours and then take her to a room. You can go in and see her then, but you can see your new son through that window," he said, pointing down the hall, "in just a few minutes." The doctor turned as he was leaving and said, "Oh, Mr. Miller, your wife says his name is Tommy. She said to tell you that." He smiled and disappeared around the corner. Kevin had unconsciously been holding his breath the whole time Dr. Campbell was speaking, and now he exhaled, releasing the longest, deepest audible sigh of relief. He stood perfectly still, like a statue, for a couple of minutes, collecting his thoughts, and then made his way down the hall toward the window where he could see his son. At precisely six o'clock in the morning, Valentine's Day, Kevin met Tommy, his beautiful seven-pound, fifteen-ounce bundle of joy with a full head of thick dark wavy hair. Tommy was sleeping soundly, just like his mother was sleeping back in the recovery room. Both were okay, and that was all that mattered.

CHAPTER 14

Home Sweet Home

By the end of March, Sarah and Kevin were accustomed to their new normal—2:00 a.m. feedings and frequent diaper changing. Sarah quit her now-part-time job so she could be a full-time mommy, and Kevin lovingly helped Sarah with the baby as much as he could; he didn't even mind changing diapers. Their months of saving before the wedding would have to support them until Tommy was at least a year old; then Sarah planned to find competent daycare for him so she could return to work.

Tommy looked adorable in his soft, blue blanket sleeper, Sarah's favourite, as he slept quietly in his crib at the foot of his parents' bed. The only unusual happening in their home lately was the occasional night when Tommy would sleep through the night, giving Sarah a full eight hours of much-needed sleep.

By August, Tommy was almost six months old and napping quietly in his stroller in the living room. Sarah tuned the television to a children's program in the event he woke up before she finished her chores. Sarah was washing lunch dishes when she smelled the unmistakable odor of cigar smoke. She remembered Kevin's confidence that the Old Spice cologne scent came through the kitchen pipes, so she immediately drained the sink and placed her nose as close to the drain as she could. There was no smoke odor.

"Very strange," she told herself. "Where is that smell coming from?" At the kitchen/hall entrance, Sarah again smelled the smoke, stronger this time. She darted quickly into the living room to check on Tommy, who was still sleeping soundly, and the cigar smell quickly dissipated. Sarah decided that it was the impish little girl spirit playing games with her. "I don't know what your name is," she said aloud, "but please, aren't you a little young to be smoking cigars?" Sarah decided to not tell Kevin about the smoke odor because she didn't want anything to disrupt their happiness.

Two weeks later, about four in the morning, she and Kevin were awakened by the sound of heavy footsteps coming from their living room. Kevin quickly grabbed his baseball bat to defend his family against the intruder. "Stay here, Sarah. Don't make a sound," he whispered almost inaudibly and quickly darted through the kitchen and hall. At the living room entrance, he suddenly stopped, partly because he felt an icy blast of freezing air and partly because dense blackness filled the windowless room. He hesitated only long enough to turn on the wall switch. The room, now flooded with light, was just as they had left it, undisturbed; no one was in the room except Kevin. He had expected to find at least a rerun of the "magazines and throw pillows" incident. Kevin called to Sarah, "Honey, it's okay. Come here."

"What is it? Who made the walking noises?" Sarah quickly assessed the living room and noted that nothing was disturbed. *Those steps were not the steps of a little girl.*

She thought to herself, *Is this another spirit?* but she said nothing; Kevin was already clearly upset. The rest of the night was spent searching the apartment for any substantial evidence of an intruder. Sarah put the coffee on, and Kevin looked into every crawl space large enough to contain a man—under the bed, in the bedroom closet, the broom closet, shower area, even the odd, three-by-six storage area in the hall where he felt another icy blast. By sunrise, Sarah accepted that their tiny apartment housed more than one spirit, a little girl and at least one unknown, probably male, possibly malicious spirit. The following month brought insomnia to both Kevin and Sarah; both understood that they must make a financially impossible move out of that house.

Two months later, as Sarah grabbed her oversized white towel and stepped out of her early morning, customarily long, relaxing shower, she sensed that someone or something was watching her, menacingly. "Is someone here?" she asked, half expecting an answer. In one smooth, seamless motion, Sarah simultaneously, skillfully wrapped her towel around her dripping body, plugged in her blow-dryer, and wiped the steamy bathroom mirror with her hand towel. Suddenly she froze, Rock of Gibraltar still. The face looking back at her from the mirror was not Sarah's. "Who are you?" she heard herself say when her normal inhale-exhale breathing returned. "What's your name?"

The man in the mirror said nothing. His sallow-cheeked death face indicated that he was very old, at least eighty years old, and his piercing black eyes sent chills down Sarah's spine. The face was surrounded by long, wiry grey hair, a long grey beard, and an equally unkempt moustache. "Why are you here?" Sarah continued, no longer expecting an answer. The silent standoff was terminated by Tommy's I-need-a-diaper-change cry in the adjacent bedroom. Sarah's eyes darted instinctively toward her baby's crib then quickly back to the mirror. The face was gone. She ran to tend to Tommy but still felt like she was being stalked by a malicious, frightening, male presence, probably one that smoked cigars. Diaper changed, Sarah returned to the bathroom to assure herself that the spirit was gone, at least temporarily. Sarah was shocked to discover the bathroom mirror covered with steam again and the fading but still legible letters D-i-e scrawled in the steam. She grabbed her Polaroid camera and took a quick picture of the mirror to show Kevin. From that day forward, she and Kevin both suspected that someone was always watching them, watching with a deep-seated hatred.

At nearly nine months old, Tommy could sit up by himself, and Sarah loved watching him play with his brightly coloured stacking blocks and other discovery toys. One afternoon, as Tommy played in the middle of his blue, thickly padded baby quilt spread on the living room floor, Sarah watched as his red, rubber ball rolled off the quilt, out of Tommy's reach, and stopped in front of the sofa. Sarah started toward the ball to retrieve it for him when it suddenly rolled back toward Tommy with enough force to clear the two-inch elevation of the quilt. The ball stopped rolling within Tommy's reach. Tommy seemed to be watching someone in the direction of the sofa, his eyes following nothing. He laughed his thank-you giggle Sarah loved so much, a giggle usually reserved for her, and Sarah suspected that Tommy was playing with the little girl spirit. Sarah wondered why the spirit was revealing herself to Tommy but not to Sarah. She began talking to the child ghost even though she couldn't see it. "Thank you for giving Tommy his ball," she said in the direction Tommy was looking, and she felt a now-familiar icy blast of air pass through her. "Looks like I scared your little friend, Tommy. Guess she doesn't want to play anymore." Sarah wondered why the child presence didn't frighten her like the old man.

The next afternoon, an unusually warm November day, Tommy was in his stroller, waiting impatiently in the living room for his mother to take him for a walk. Sarah was in the bathroom, putting the finishing touches on her makeup when she heard Tommy cry his "I don't like this" message. "I'm coming, honey. Just one more minute and we'll go walking." His impatient cries grew louder. "I'll be right there, Tommy." Sarah smiled as she thought of the child presence possibly entertaining Tommy for a few minutes, and at that moment, Tommy stopped crying. "Thank you for helping me," she said aloud to nobody and hurried toward the living room, expecting Tommy to be enjoying the company of his new friend.

In the hall, a thick, almost-palpable, heavy unmistakable smell of cigar smoke almost choked her. "Oh no." Sarah cried, "What's going on?" as she hurried into the living room. She was greeted by the stone-cold terrifying stare of the old man seated on the sofa, gently rocking Tommy in his stroller. The old man said nothing, but his message was clear. Sarah's presence was being challenged; the old man wanted them out of his territory. Sarah knew she had to get Tommy out of the house, now! "Get away from my baby!" she screamed. The confidence in her own voice surprised Sarah as she confronted the terrifying old man. Even the old man was surprised; he hadn't anticipated so much opposition. Previous tenants usually moved out after a couple of cold-spot incidents, and he didn't understand the present intruders at all.

Sarah grabbed her baby out of the stroller and rushed out, leaving a very perplexed apparition holding on to Tommy's stroller. She didn't know where she was going; she only knew that she was putting distance between herself and the ghastly old man. She wondered what the connection was between the old man and the little girl presence as she ran down the street toward the university campus. She had to find Kevin; maybe he would know what to do. She remembered the last time she felt so helpless, when Father Mitchell exiled her great-aunt Melissa back to the spirit hinterlands, wherever that was. Sarah wished the old man would somehow join her aunt and stop disrupting Kevin's and her life.

I bet those two would like each other, she thought. *That would be a marriage made in . . .* Sarah briefly enjoyed the thought.

CHAPTER 15

Exorcism

"Kevin!" Sarah called to him as she spotted him crossing the campus with some other students. "Kevin!" He turned and started walking toward her. "You will never believe what happened!" Sarah said even before Kevin reached them.

"What's going on, Sarah? Why didn't you put Tommy in his stroller?" he asked and reached to retrieve the child from her arms. "He must be getting awfully heavy for you."

"Oh, Kevin, it was terrible. We have an old man spirit in our apartment! I am so afraid of him! He was rocking Tommy in his stroller. Oh, Kevin, you should have seen him! His eyes were evil, just pure evil!" Sarah realized that she was secretly glad Kevin hadn't seen the old man and added, "But I am glad you weren't home."

"Now, what do we do?" Kevin asked when Sarah finished talking. He never doubted Sarah for a second. His mind was racing; he remembered Sarah's bathroom experience, the ominous message scrawled on the mirror, and the heavy footsteps in the living room. He had learned long ago to never doubt what Sarah told him and now feared for his family's safety. He accepted that a ghost—a very frightening, malicious, evil old man ghost—inhabited their home. Obviously, they couldn't return home, at least not today, but their limited finances limited their choices.

"I don't know what we do now, but I think we need to call Father Mitchell," Sarah urged. "For tonight, maybe we can go to a motel. Maybe Father Mitchell can be here by tomorrow morning. He'll tell us what to do!"

"Do you still have his number?"

"No, I don't, but I can get it from Dad," then she added, "With me as his daughter, I think Dad probably has his priest on speed dial."

*   *   *

The young family spent a fitful night at the first motel they could find. Sarah called Father Mitchell who agreed to come as soon as possible, and he did. The old priest surprised Kevin and Sarah when he knocked on their motel-room door early the next morning, even before they were out of bed. Father Mitchell remembered Sarah's sensitivity in supernatural affairs from his experience with Great-Aunt Melissa and knew the urgency in Sarah's voice was sincere.

He listened carefully as they explained about the mischievous child and malevolent old entity who had taken up residence in their attic apartment. It did not take much convincing. "We've got to get busy," he explained. "From what you've told me, the male spirit is gaining strength. We must do an exorcism." He took a long, deep breath, letting it out slowly before continuing. "What time is checkout?"

"I think it is 11:00 a.m. Why?" Kevin asked.

"I'll be back by then. Stay here until I come to get you, okay? I've got to get a few things." With that, Father Mitchell hurried out the door, his rapid footsteps on the concrete parking lot indicating his sense of urgency.

True to his word, the priest was back about 10:30 a.m.; he carried a briefcase full of papers, a vial of holy water, and a rather large ivory cross. "Are you ready?" Kevin nodded. Sarah was busy tending to Tommy, but she too nodded her head in agreement. "Let's go. The sooner we get started, the sooner we'll be finished, and you three can have your home back." They piled into Father Mitchell's Volkswagen and anxiously sped back to their apartment.

After sprinkling holy water across the threshold, Father Mitchell was the first to enter. As he climbed the stairs, he began what he called his most powerful exorcism prayer to purify and protect a home. He held the cross in front of his chest as he began. "In the name of Jesus Christ, our God and Lord, strengthened by the intercession of the immaculate virgin, Mary, Mother of God, of Blessed Michael the Archangel, of the blessed apostles Peter and Paul, and all the saints, we confidently undertake to repulse the attacks and deceits of the devil."

By the time Father Mitchell finished speaking, he had reached the dark living room. Sarah held Tommy close as she and Kevin followed the priest. Sarah reached around the door frame and turned on the light, flooding the windowless room with light. Sarah was the first to see the old man glaring at them from the sofa. He was invisible to both Kevin and Father Mitchell. Nevertheless, the priest continued, "God arises, his enemies are scattered, and those who hate him flee before him." The cross became suddenly burning hot, and Father Mitchell's grip loosened briefly, but he managed to hold on to it. Sarah and Kevin simultaneously crossed their hearts.

"Sarah! I can see the old man," Kevin said pointing toward the sofa. "Father, do you see him?" Father Mitchell nodded his head and motioned with his finger that Kevin should stay silent until the exorcism was finished.

Kevin watched in amazement as the apparition quickly gained form, growing from a hazy mist to an almost tangible, empirical being. Father Mitchell continued, "We drive you from us, whoever you may be, unclean spirits, all satanic posers, and all infernal invaders. God the Father commands you." He raised the cross above his head and lowered it. "God the Son commands you," and he repeated the cross movement. "God the Holy Spirit commands you." Again, he moved the cross up and down. "Christ, God's Word made flesh, commands you. The sacred sign of the cross commands you, as does also the power of the mysteries of the Christian faith." However, when Father Mitchell raised the cross again, the apparition began shimmering, vaporizing like an oasis losing substance as one nears it. "The glorious Mother of God, the Virgin Mary, commands you," and he raised the cross again, this time holding it high as he continued. "The faith of the holy apostles Peter and Paul and the other apostles commands you. You have been rendered powerless and are banished. Leave this home now and forever."

When Father Mitchell lowered the cross back down to his chest, the spirit's face grimaced as though in extreme agony but emitted no sound. Instead, it silently disappeared, evaporating into thin air. "We thank you, Lord, King of Ages, for this through the intercession of our most blessed, glorious lady, Mary, ever virgin, Mother of God, of the most splendid archangels and all your saints."

Incredulously Sarah asked, "Is that it, Father? Is he gone, gone for good?" Sarah was amazed at how fast and easy the exorcism had been. She had half-expected a do-over of William Peter Blatty's *The Exorcist*, complete with demonic screams and green pea soup, although the calm and peace Sarah now felt assured her that the evil entity was indeed gone.

Father Mitchell smiled slightly, "Yes, Sarah, he is gone, but I expect the little girl is still here. We may need to use a different kind of prayer for the child." The old priest's smile widened to involve his whole face, and he continued, "Pun intended, the Vatican wasn't built in a day, so for now, looks like it's one down, one to go. We'll tend to the little miss at a later date, okay?"

"Thank you, Father," Kevin smiled too. "You have given us back our home." He turned off the light after Sarah, Tommy, and Father Mitchell left the room, but the room was no longer consumed with the dense black-hole blackness they had accepted as normal. Instead, the room seemed to glow slightly like it too was thanking the priest. That night, everyone slept peacefully.

*   *   *

Early the next morning, since Kevin didn't have any classes, Sarah asked him to babysit Tommy while she visited the local newspaper office. She wanted to know more about their home and thought she might discover some information in the newspaper's archived microfiche files.

After several hours of scrolling through approximately ten years of dizzying, eye-numbing microfiche files, Sarah finally found it, a news article about a man found dead in his apartment, now her apartment.

"Kitchener-Waterloo police found sixty-two-year-old John Fitzhugh deceased in his Waterloo apartment at 4500 Woolwich Court, North today," Detective Stephen Smith said.

The landlady, Judith Gentry, concerned for Fitzhugh's welfare after no one reported seeing him for almost six weeks, discovered the body yesterday and notified the authorities.

"The body has been sent for autopsy, but the cause of death is expected to be natural causes," Smith said.

Fitzhugh was granted sole custody of his four-year-old granddaughter, Lucy Fitzhugh, one year ago following the disappearance of his daughter, the child's mother, and the death of his Fitzhugh's wife, Laura. Fitzhugh reported the child was abducted from their backyard two months ago by an unknown individual.

Police are still investigating the abduction.

Sarah continued scrolling for two more hours but found nothing more about the Fitzhugh family. "I have to find more information about the little girl, Lucy. She must be the child in the photograph," she said aloud. Her mind raced with a plethora of questions for which she had no answers. *Why is Lucy a ghost? Why is she still in the apartment? The story says she was abducted, by whom? Why? Now at least we know who she is, but where is she, and more importantly, how did she die?*
Determined to find answers, Sarah hurried home to share what she learned with Kevin. *He'll know what to do next. He always does,* she told herself.

* * *

Kevin was surprised to see Sarah so upset again. He hoped the exorcism took care of their immediate problems. Usually, Sarah was incredibly calm especially when things were off-the-wall weird. He listened to her litany of questions without interrupting her. When Sarah finally paused to inhale, he interjected, "Honey, what did you say the officer's name is, the man that found the body?"

"I think it said Detective Smith," Sarah explained. "Are you going to talk to him? Oh, Kevin, I think that's a wonderful idea. I hope he still works for the department. When can you go? Do you want me to go too?"

One quick phone call and Kevin had a four o'clock appointment with Detective Smith who remembered the case very well; Lucy's abduction was the only unsolved case in his file. In fact, Smith recalled every detail about the afternoon abduction and, later, the old man's death. "Fitzhugh was found lying on the floor in a narrow hallway. He had a death grip on the knob of a long empty wall cabinet built close to the floor," Smith told Kevin. "It was the strangest cupboard I've ever seen, almost big enough to hold a man, strange, very strange cupboard!" He paused for a moment and continued, "Is that cupboard still there? Have you seen it?" Kevin nodded agreement to both questions. Then Smith added, "You know, I always suspected Fitzhugh of being involved in Lucy's disappearance."

Kevin suddenly felt like he was in an avalanche of puzzle pieces falling into place, creating a clear cathartic vision in his mind. He recalled the night when he and Sarah heard footsteps in their apartment and the blast of cold air he felt when he investigated the strange three-by-six floor closet. "Did the investigators ever take the cupboard apart? I have a very strange feeling that it holds the key, the answers we need."

Thirty minutes later, Sarah watched from the living room doorway as two police officers dismantled the floor cabinet, first removing all their personal belongings and then removing the single shelf. Next, they removed the bottom, the floor of the closet. At first, it looked like a large kitty-litter box below the floorboard; someone had filled the space with several inches of cat litter. As police began searching the litter, one of them announced, "We found something, sir. I think it's a child's remains. Better bring in the detectives."

Sarah heard the officer's announcement, but she wasn't watching any longer. Her attention was on the glowing figure of a little girl, Lucy, smiling peacefully at her from the corner of their living room. "Thank you, Sarah. Good-bye," the child whispered, her voice sounding like the flutter of a million butterflies' wings, as a brilliant, calming light suddenly engulfed Lucy's image and both Lucy and the light disappeared together.

After Fitzhugh's expulsion and Lucy's release, there were no more spirit encounters in the apartment. The Miller household belonged to only Kevin, Sarah, and Tommy. Home, sweet home, finally.

Chapter 16

Picture It

For the first time since Sarah was eight years old, life was normal. She didn't sense anyone surreptitiously watching her as she cooked, cleaned, bathed, and took care of Tommy—in short, she enjoyed the freedom of a "spirit" less life, a life without mystery or fear. She happily busied herself with Suzy Homemaker activities, painting ceramics, knitting Tommy a popular Canadian-style fisherman-knit pullover, and exploring other crafts, but her absolute favourite project soon became creating a family photo album for Tommy.

Ruby brought several shoe boxes full of black-and-white photographs of Sarah's childhood, and they spent several enjoyable mother-daughter afternoons together sorting and organizing the pictures. One afternoon, Ruby suggested that Sarah should ask Gloria for photos of Kevin's childhood, and Gloria was thrilled to share her son's pictorial childhood. It became a group project; all three women literally traveled back in time via photographs. Every photo had an inherent story, and every story insisted that it be heard.

Sarah's photos added another dimension to the album—wedding photos, Tommy's baby pictures, Christmas, and their first Thanksgiving as a family. One afternoon, in preparation for her two moms, as she called them, Sarah spread the Thanksgiving photos out on the kitchen table. One stood out from the mix; Sarah found the photograph where she and Kevin first discovered Lucy, the impish, dark-haired four-year-old girl wearing white peeking around the corner, but the child was no longer in the photograph. It was as if Lucy had never been there. "I hope you are happy wherever you are, Lucy," Sarah said aloud and smiled. "You may be gone, but you are definitely not forgotten."

Later that afternoon, as the three women dug through yet another shoe box of photos, Sarah suddenly gasped. Mentally, Sarah was instantly transported back to a time when she was a desperately ill eight-year-old child staring into the eyes of a lady in red seated at the foot of her bed. Physically, she was staring into the same eyes; only now, they stared back at her in black-and-white from the worn photograph in her hand.

"What's the matter, honey?" Ruby asked. "You look like you have just seen a ghost." Her attempt to lighten the mood fell on deaf ears because Sarah didn't hear her. She stared raptly at the haunting eyes in the photograph. Even in the photo's worn condition, those eyes were unmistakable.

"Who is this woman?" she finally managed to ask Gloria.

"Oh my," Gloria said leaning forward to take a closer look. "That is a picture of my mother. I never met her because she passed away when I was born," she paused briefly, "literally died giving me life. Wasn't she beautiful?" Gloria again paused pensively. "I'm told that she always wore red. All her clothes were red. I guess it was her favourite colour." Gloria paused briefly to study Sarah's puzzled expression. "Why do you ask, dear? Does she look familiar to you?"

"Actually, she looks like someone I've known almost my whole life. I think she's my guardian angel."

SHORT STORY

SISTERHOOD

Two o'clock in the morning and she was still awake. Carol's insomnia was getting worse. She added up her total number of sleep hours during the past week and lost count somewhere around thirty hours. Carol Palmer tried to pinpoint the exact day, week, or month that her life had fallen apart.

Carol was the only child born to her mother. She was born out of wedlock, and her mother gave the infant almost immediately into her own mother's care, Grandmother Sara, before leaving town. Grandma Sara unceremoniously became Carol's mother.

The name given to Carol at birth foreshadowed a life of surreal unhappiness. Her mother chose to name the infant Carol Rose Ann Palmer, a name inappropriately longer than her eighteen-inch-long birth body but an appropriate length for her thirty-five years of relatively good health. Life was full of promise and should have been good for Carol, but happiness seemed to always be just beyond her reach.

Ironically, Carol's initials, CRAP, said it all; her initials both foreshadowed and symbolized her life. Carol's introversion kept her from making any friends in school. She finished high school but had to leave college to take care of her ailing grandmother who had lung cancer. Grandmother Sara's cancer metastasized slowly over the next seven years, and she inevitably passed away.

For almost a year, Carol was free to live her own life. She saw movies, ate in restaurants, smiled at fellow shoppers at the local K-Mart, and worked full-time at the neighbourhood McDonald's. Her shyness would not permit actual conversations with nonfamily.

Eleven months passed, and her life was once again put on the back burner. Carol had to take care of Grandpa Jim whose almost nine-year descent in senile dementia now required all of Carol's attention. She cooked for him, cleaned up after him, chauffeured him to and from the doctor's office, washed his clothing and bedding, and later, even changed his diapers.

Insomnia began to torment Carol. Minor daytime worries became overwhelming nighttime problems. Carol needed help—some kind of divine intervention.

How she longed for friends—real friends—not the pretend friends of *Days of Our Lives, The Young and the*

Restless, and *All My Children.* Although Carol believed she knew these soap stars intimately, they were only acquaintances. After all, Carol reasoned, "I'm not crazy! I'm just lonely." Carol wanted to sit down and enjoy an afternoon cup of tea with a real friend, somebody with whom she could share a confidence or a laugh.

Usually, Carol was preoccupied with Grandpa Jim's medical and physical needs. Rarely did she think much about herself. However, one afternoon, after Grandpa Jim drifted off into troubled, medication-induced sleep, Carol gave full attention to her own situation. *Soap's personas always find solutions for their over dramatized problems,* she thought. Sometimes they develop imaginary friends. "I have no friends," she said out loud and laughed at hearing herself summarily analyze the essence of her problem. "I have no friends," she said a little louder, and again, "I have no friends!" raising her voice to a high-pitched scream. It felt good, real good.

So how do I make friends? she thought to herself. *I am housebound.* Immediately she felt guilty for being self-centered and scolded herself aloud, "I love Grandpa and will always take care of him. He's my pseudo dad."

In a moment of cathartic revelation, the solution came to her in an inaudible whisper from somewhere deep within herself. The answer had been within her all her life. "I need friends. Why not have pseudo friends? I am Carol Rose Ann Palmer. Why not make friends with myself?" and she laughed aloud at the simplicity of her solution.

She knew about multiple personalities. These were alter egos that arose involuntarily in one host body. What about alter egos that were consciously, deliberately created by the host? "I can make friends, real friends, within myself," she heard herself say. Almost immediately, she heard herself respond, "What I need is a video, a cold Dr. Pepper, and a bowl of buttered popcorn."

"I think I'll make Rose the party girl," Carol laughed as the "two" of them tossed a bag of popcorn into the microwave. Rose chose to watch *Gone with the Wind*, and both Rose and Carol cried when Rhett Butler declared, "Frankly, my dear, I just don't give a damn." That night, Carol's dreams were somehow less lonely.

For the next few days, Carol thought often about her new "friend," Rose, especially when feelings of depression and self-pity weighed heavy upon her. Carol blushed when she remembered her grandmother saying, "It's okay to ask yourself questions, but be careful when you start hearing answers." Carol decided to break off the friendship with Rose.

Then the bill collectors began calling. Grandpa Jim had insisted on taking care of the monthly bills and angrily refused to give up the responsibility. As dementia deepened, finances worsened, and Carol once again needed help, a friend's help. She needed distance emotionally, a step back from her problems. Carol turned to Ann.

"Hello," Carol answered the telephone. "Yes, this is Carol Palmer."

"This is Jim Crawford with the public utility company," a crisp impersonal voice said. "I'm calling because your household is scheduled for service interruption tomorrow unless you arrange payment on your account today."

Carol could feel her face flush with anger, embarrassment, and shyness. Before she could fully comprehend what she was saying, Carol heard her voice say, "Just a minute. I'll get my financial advisor, Ann."

Crawford never noticed the similarity between Carol's and Ann's voices, or at least he never mentioned it. Ann skillfully worked out a payment schedule and service went on uninterrupted. Ann thus became the family bill payer, the financial advisor, and the telephone consultant.

Carol smiled at her clever problem-solving strategy. After that, Carol, Ann, and Rose became close friends, often having lengthy three-way conversations. They shared the same likes and dislikes, thoughts and concerns—a special sisterhood. Carol was no longer alone. She wasn't even shy around her new friends; after all, they were all family. Every afternoon, Carol, Rose, and Ann shared a cup of tea and a laugh.

Then Grandpa Jim died, suddenly and unexpectedly, during one of his afternoon naps. Neighbours began a sporadic two-day procession of green bean casseroles and sliced ham. Ten o'clock the night before Grandpa's funeral, Carol, Rose, and Ann were startled when the doorbell rang.

"Um, Carol?" the woman stammered. "I—I'm—your mother," she added bashfully as she raised her bowed head and subconsciously brushed a length of wispy salt-and-pepper hair from her forehead. "I've been too ashamed to come back for you," she sobbed. "Thirty-five years ago I gave birth to you, and—I finally—I'm back. Can you ever forgive . . . ?" Her words disappeared into an incoherent, inconsistent, all-consuming sadness. It was as though her mother's well-planned speech was literally being devoured, chewed up, and swallowed. Her shoulders shook with emotion, causing the tears to form an interesting crisscross pattern on her cheeks. Carol unintentionally studied the woman's features, as though she was trying to see deep into her mother's soul.

After several minutes of awkward silence, a smile began to form in the corners of Carol's mouth and spread slowly, intermittently across Carol's face, as though the smile didn't exactly know where to begin, where to end, or even whether to exist at all. Carol thought a moment, *Another family member means I have a new friend.* Carol finally heard herself say "Mom," and she liked the sound of the word, so she repeated it. "Mom, did you know that you have triplets?"

CPSIA information can be obtained at www.ICGtesting.com
Printed in the USA
LVOW06*0908200514

386553LV00002B/10/P